ADVENTURE
QUEST

Danger at Half-Moon Lake

by Joan Rawlins Biggar

Illustrated by Kay Salem

Concordia

Publishing House
St. Louis

Scripture quotations in this publication are from The Holy Bible: NEW INTERNATIONAL VERSION, © 1973, 1978, 1984 by the International Bible Society. Used by permission of Zondervan Bible Publishers.

Copyright © 1991 Concordia Publishing House
3558 S. Jefferson Avenue, St. Louis, MO 63118-3968
Manufactured in the United States of America

Library of Congress Cataloging-in-Publication Data

Biggar, Joan Rawlins, 1936–
    Danger at Half-Moon Lake/by Joan Rawlins Biggar.
    (Adventure quest)
    Summary: Thirteen-year-old Billy, visiting his pastor uncle in Alaska, befriends an orphaned native Alaskan boy and together they break a liquor smuggling ring.
    ISBN 0-570-04194-5
    1. Eskimos—Juvenile fiction. [1. Eskimos—Fiction. 2. Indians of North America—Alaska—Fiction. 3. Alaska—Fiction. 4. Adventure and adventurers—Fiction. 5. Christian life—Fiction.] I. Title. II. Series: Biggar, Joan Rawlins, 1936– Aventure quest.
    PZ7.B483Ad 1991
[Fic]—dc20   90-2383
1 2 3 4 5 6 7 8 9 10 00 99 98 97 96 95 94 93 92 91

To Bob
my husband, friend
and favorite Alaskan

Adventure Quest Series

Treasure at Morning Gulch
Danger at Half-Moon Lake

Contents

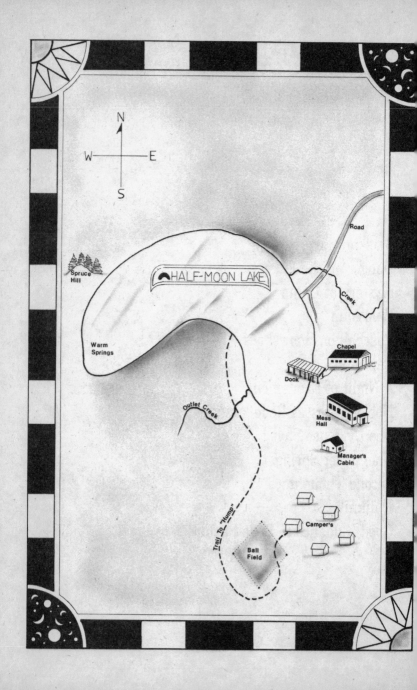

Alaskan Surprises

"I can't believe it's spring back home in Washington!" Thirteen-year-old Billy Skarson's words blew away on the icy air.

Uncle Jess Cassidy chuckled. He shouted back, "This *is* spring for Alaska!"

Billy ducked his head against his uncle's shoulders. But that made his glasses press like super-cooled bars of iron against his numb cheeks. Sure that his ears had turned to slabs of ice, he pulled his parka hood up over the spiky orange hair sticking out from under his cap.

The snowmachine sputtered, and slowed for a wooden bridge across the creek. Billy twisted to watch a team of huskies round the curve of the creek bed behind them.

He wrinkled his freckled nose as the dogsled drew nearer. That stuck-up Indian kid who stayed with Uncle Jess rode the runners of the wood and rawhide sled. What was his name? Moses Paul? No, Paul Moses.

Last night, soon after arriving at the Cassidy's

house from the Fairbanks airport, Billy had tried to get acquainted. Paul answered a couple of his questions with a yes or no. But when Billy asked about his school, Paul didn't answer. He might as well have talked to the wall.

Now Uncle Jess, sturdy and rosy-cheeked like his nephew, pointed to show Paul the direction. He gunned the snowmobile up the creek bank and across the drifted-over bridge, then headed between ranks of bare willows and birch toward an expanse of blinding white.

"Here's Half-Moon Lake," Uncle Jess shouted. "We'll take a shortcut." The boy tightened his grip on the man's parka as the machine bounced over ridges and down to the snow-covered ice. To the right, scrubby trees swept around in a curve to mark the shore. The lake's far end was hidden by a point of land jutting out to make the inside of the "half-moon." Beyond that rose a high, rounded hill.

The machine swung left. Billy saw no sign of human presence except for an unfinished-looking square building. *That* couldn't be the Bible camp, could it?

The snowmachine coasted to a stop as his uncle cut the engine. In the sudden silence, Billy heard the squeak of sled runners and the panting of dogs. "Whoa," grunted Paul as he hopped from the back of the sled. Running forward, he held the lead dog to keep the team from tangling the harnesses.

Jess Cassidy rubbed his sheepskin mittens together, beaming. "The good Lord couldn't have given us a nicer day to start new work for Him! Billy, I'm sure glad you were willing to use your spring break to help us out."

8

Billy stared at the ugly plywood building. He'd expected a cozy cabin where they could warm up in front of a roaring fire. "Is *this* the camp?"

Uncle Jess's booming laugh came from deep inside his ample midsection. "I told you it was primitive. But remember, you can't see much with everything under a foot of snow."

He motioned toward a long, drifted rectangle frozen into the lake. "That's the dock. Needs repair. This building's the main hall, for chapel and other get-togethers. Up there's the mess hall."

Billy hoisted himself off the snowmachine. Now he saw the long, low building half-hidden in the trees.

"We'll start on the mess hall today. The kids will come day after tomorrow to work on the chapel building."

Uncle Jess pastored the Log Cabin Chapel in Fairbanks. Last night several teenagers from the church had stopped by the house for some last minute planning. A small blond about Billy's age flashed him a mischievous grin as they left. Would she be along?

"We'll stay in the manager's cabin," Uncle Jess continued. "The campers' cabins are farther up, in the woods. There's a ball field, too. You boys can go exploring after we get the sled unloaded."

Billy glanced at Paul standing by the lead dog, his brown face unsmiling. Exploring with that woodenhead? What fun!

"One warning," the pastor went on. "Two weeks ago the men from our camp committee found signs that some of the cabins had been entered. Probably only

9

snowmobilers poking around, but let me know if you see anything unusual."

Uncle Jess turned toward his foster son. "Paul, the manager's cabin is just past the mess hall. Want to take the sled up there and stake out the dogs? We'll be right behind you."

Paul nodded. He gave a low whistle. The dogs followed him up the bank, straining against their harnesses as they broke through the crusted snow.

"What do you think of that, Bill?" queried the man. "Did you ever think you'd see a real, working dogsled?"

"It's great," Billy answered. The scene reminded him of a Jack London story he'd seen on a video at school. But why was Paul so unfriendly? As if reading his thoughts, Uncle Jess lowered his voice.

"When I wrote you about coming north, Billy, we didn't know we'd have Paul. But I'm sure the Lord has something special in mind for this week. That boy really needs a friend."

Uh, oh, thought Billy. What was it cousin Jodi said last summer when they talked about living as Christians? That because Jesus loves us, He expects us to love others? But Paul so far had barely spoken. It would be hard to even *like* him.

"Why did Paul come to live with you?" he asked.

"Same reason most of our foster kids come. Alcohol." They watched Paul disappear with the sled around the corner of the mess hall. "Paul comes from Kuliknik, one of the villages up north on the Yukon. His mother died when he was very young. He moved with his dad to their trapping cabin in the bush. He's fourteen, but he's only had about three years of school."

10

"Only three years of school!" Billy's eyes blinked and popped open. "They'd never let us get away with that in Washington!"

"There was no school where they were trapping. Paul's father tried hard, but whenever he went to the village, the booze smugglers got to him. Kuliknik is dry. That means the villagers voted not to allow liquor there, but some people sneak it in anyway. One night last December Mr. Moses was drinking. He fell in a snowbank, going home, and froze to death."

Billy felt like someone had hit him in the middle. The pain of his own mother's death several years before rushed back as his uncle continued.

"No one had room to keep Paul for long. Just two weeks ago, the missionary in the village sent him to us. He's having a tough time. The city can overwhelm people who've spent their lives in the bush." Uncle Jess paused. "Then the school put him in the fourth grade. You can imagine how he feels about that."

No wonder Paul wouldn't talk about school. Billy didn't know what to say. He still had his father, and he had the Marshes: his aunt and uncle and Mike and Jodi. Mike and Jodi helped him catch up in school after he and Dad moved to Washington from their old home in Montana. Imagine a fourteen-year-old in a class with fourth-graders!

Uncle Jess tried to restart the snowmobile. The engine sputtered, coughed, then died.

"C'mon, Bill," he said. "We'll come back later to tinker with it."

The back of the mess hall sat flush against the slope of the land, its front end supported by pilings.

11

This made a storage place for several overturned rowboats. Through the space between the building and the rowboats Billy glimpsed Paul tying the dogs, each to its own tree or bush.

Beyond, a small log building, the manager's cabin, lay nestled under some spruce trees. Uncle Jess opened the shutters that protected the windows on either side of the door and brushed the snow off the step.

Billy carried bundles from the sled into the one-room cabin. "Look, there're frost crystals on the walls," he said.

Two sets of double bunks filled the back wall. A four-legged, oil-barrel stove squatted in the center of the room, its stovepipe reaching up through the ceiling.

The door in the end of the barrel creaked as Uncle Jess looked inside. He banged the stovepipe. "Looks like it works okay. We'll light a fire to thaw this place out, as soon as we find some wood."

Just then Paul thumped through the door with an armload of dead spruce branches. "For kindling," he told his foster father. "Wood pile—behind cabin."

He went to bring in some firewood. Billy followed him. The huskies lay in the snow, still panting from their run. He started toward the nearest animal, wanting to make friends.

"Stop!" Paul's command startled him. "That Devil. He mean. Sometime bite."

Billy took a closer look at the pointed face with the white mask and slanted blue eyes. As a rumble started in the husky's throat he quickly retreated.

"These working dogs. No pet!" Paul's black eyes were scornful.

12

Billy felt his face burning. What made this guy think he was so smart? He couldn't even talk right! He grabbed an armful of wood and followed Paul into the cabin.

Soon a fire crackled in the barrel. Melting snow sizzled in a pot. They'd have hot chocolate shortly. His resentment subsiding, Billy shrugged out of his heavy parka. He looked around. There was more stuff in here than he'd first thought . . . pots and pans in a cabinet under a window, hatchet and saw hanging on nails. And up above the door . . . a pair of skis, the wide, old-fashioned wooden kind with cable bindings.

He climbed on a chair to lift them down. "Hey, Paul, if we had some poles we could have some fun!" The Indian boy watched, expressionless.

"Ever tried skijoring?" asked Uncle Jess.

"What's that?" Billy had been skiing only once, when he'd gone with the Marsh family and his dad to Steven's Pass last Christmas. He'd spent more time in the snow than on it, and that was *with* ski poles.

"You don't need poles for skijoring. You fasten a rope to a dog's harness and let him pull you where you want to go."

Paul brightened. "My dog Koolaa . . . me and him did that."

"Where's Koolaa now?" Billy asked curiously.

"Gave neighbor. Him take care." Paul's face closed up again.

"Molly, my lead dog, loves skijoring. Why don't you boys try it while I get the work laid out in the mess hall?" suggested Jess.

Molly was a large black husky with white face and

13

throat. The markings arching above her eyes gave her a friendly, questioning expression, and her brush of a tail wagged a greeting. She trotted ahead of them to the lake, tail curled cheerfully over her back.

"I show you," Paul said as he buckled on her harness and attached a length of rope. He adjusted the bindings of the old-fashioned skis to fit his boots, picked up the loop at the end of the rope, and whistled. Molly started off at a trot across the crusted snow.

Paul glided behind, leaving parallel tracks on the surface of the lake to mark his swoops and turns. He turned the dog when they reached the far side of the lake, and skimmed back to where Billy waited by the broken-down snowmobile.

Excitement made Billy's fingers fumble as he bent to adjust the bindings. Skijoring looked easy, and fun!

"Go slow 'til you used to it."

Billy whistled to Molly as Paul had done. The dog leaped ahead. The rope jerked tight, and the snow came up to meet Billy with a whump! Molly looked around, puzzled.

"Not as easy as it looked," Billy mumbled, getting to his feet. Was that amusement in Paul's black eyes? But he said nothing, just brought Molly back and held out the end of the rope.

Billy snatched it ungraciously. This time he leaned back against the rope as it tightened. He felt himself moving effortlessly out onto the lake. He whistled again and Molly trotted faster.

He leaned to the side as Paul had done. Sure enough, he swung in the opposite direction. This was as good as flying!

14

He leaned the other way, further this time, and found himself again plowing head first through the snow. This time he hung on to the rope, yelling "Whoa." Molly stopped and he struggled up, digging snow from inside the neck of his parka. He glanced over his shoulder. Paul had the cowl off the snowmobile and was bending over the engine.

Molly again leaned into the harness, running strong and smooth. The sun shone blindingly bright out here in the open, and the air bit his face. Billy pulled his cap down further to shield his eyes as they rounded the curve in the middle of the half-moon and headed for the other end of the lake.

This was great! Molly looked back, red tongue flapping.

"Go, Molly, Go!" he shouted. His skis traced graceful S curves over the sparkling snow. Frosty crystals flew up and settled with hissing sounds as he passed.

Maybe he should go back now so Paul could have another turn. No, he thought, remembering Paul's amusement at his spill. Let him wait.

A white path ran straight up the hill ahead of him, like a power-line clearing, only he could see no wires. It seemed to start near the lake shore.

"Maybe we can ski up there . . . wonder if it's a road?" he said to himself. "Haw," he yelled to Molly. "No, I mean, Gee!" The dog swung first left, then right. They skimmed across the lake toward the line through the trees.

Suddenly Billy's heart nearly stopped. A booming c-r-a-c-k sounded beneath his flying skis.

15

Danger on the Lake

Molly veered sharply. Billy struggled to stay upright on the clumsy, old-fashioned skis. He strained to hear further sounds from the ice through the blood pounding in his ears. Looking over his shoulder, he saw now that the snow he'd just crossed looked discolored in spots and not as smooth as the rest of the lake.

His arms screamed for rest. He yelled for Molly to stop, and stood for a few minutes while his racing heart slowed. From here he could not see Paul or the camp. He and the sled dog were all alone except for two big black birds flapping across the blue-china bowl of sky. He marveled at the untouched feeling of this frozen world. This was Paul's world, but the strange, frozen beauty hadn't kept ugliness and sadness out of his life.

He signaled Molly to go on. How would he, Billy, react if people looked down on him just because he came from a different background? How would he like to be in class with children five years younger than himself?

16

Billy remembered how miserable his own life had been after his mother had died. He was always in trouble with his dad for not paying attention in school and for getting behind. Then Aunt Adele and Uncle Alan had adopted them into their family. His cousins, Mike and Jodi, had helped him get caught up at school. And Jodi had reminded him how much God loved him—enough to send His own Son to die on the cross to pay the price for his sins. How could he share all that with Paul?

As Billy rounded the hump in the middle of the lake, he saw Paul still bending over the engine. He halted Molly beside the snowmachine.

"Sorry I took such a long turn."

The Indian boy barely glanced up. He slammed the cowling. "Maybe it run now," he said. Before Billy could mention the frightening noise on the ice, Paul jumped onto the machine and turned the key. The engine sprang to life with a throaty roar, then idled smoothly.

"Hey, not bad!" came a shout from near the mess hall. Uncle Jess stood beaming. "Go ahead, Paul, take it out and see how it runs."

Paul lifted his hand in acknowledgment and gunned the machine away from the bank. He ran it in a big oval out on the lake, slowing, then speeding up. Billy scowled, his good resolve forgotten. The showoff! He thought of the many times he'd helped his dad repair engines in his business, the Bayside Garage. "I could probably have fixed it myself," he muttered.

The other boy brought the machine in fast, braking with a flourish so the rear end whipped around. Uncle Jess clapped him on the back. "Good job!" Paul ducked

17

his head, but he looked pleased. "Come on now, both of you guys. It's time to go to work."

Billy's glasses clouded over as the warm air of the mess hall hit them. The cold lenses turned the mist to ice. He tipped his head to look over the top of the rims as Uncle Jess explained the work to be done.

He gave the boys a pry bar and hammers and set them to tearing out a wall that separated two long, narrow rooms. "Pull out one board at a time. Use the hammer to remove the nails. We'll save the good stuff to use again." He showed them how to do it.

Billy attacked the next board with the pry bar. "Ouch!"

A long sliver of wood splintered from the edge of the board, drawing blood from a knuckle that got in the way.

"Easy now. One end loose, then the other."

"Got it." Billy pulled the board free and gave it to Paul, who pounded out the nails.

"With this wall out, we'll have a nice large dining room," the pastor said.

"What happened to the people who used to run this camp?" asked Billy.

"They joined some Anchorage churches to start a bigger camp down near Denali Park. But this camp suits us just fine. Our Log Cabin Chapel is part of a mission group that works in the northern bush. We wanted a camp for our local kids and for village kids who have no camp of their own."

Jess started for the kitchen, where he'd been sawing boards for cupboard shelves. He pushed up the sliding door that closed off the pass-through between

18

kitchen and dining room. "This old camp will be as good as any in the Lower Forty-eight when we get through with it!"

The boys tore the boards loose, one at a time, then stacked them. They fed the shortest pieces to the crackling fire in the big stone fireplace. Neither spoke.

Presently the silence began to bother Billy.

"What's it like, living in the bush?" he asked.

Paul grunted as he pried a nail from a board. "Good. No school. No books. No questions."

Billy tried again. "I didn't like school either when Dad and I came to live with my cousins. They helped me catch up in the subjects I was failing."

"I no need help. No need books to hunt and trap."

"Don't you like living with Uncle Jess?"

"He okay. Not like some white men. They come village. Bring whiskey. Then make fun of Indian. Take land, shoot animals. But it worse, in town."

That was a long speech for Paul. Billy didn't know how to answer. He worked in silence for a while. Paul muttered something under his breath, so low Billy wasn't sure he understood. "I go home," he thought he heard.

Finally they tore off the last board, leaving only the bare studs standing in a row down the middle of one big new room.

At five o'clock Paul went to feed the dogs. In the kitchen, Billy grabbed a hammer to help nail down a new plywood counter top. Over the pounding of their hammers, Uncle Jess yelled, "We're nearly done with this. Why don't you get the frankfurters and potato salad we brought for dinner? We'll use your nice fire to roast our hot dogs."

Billy put on his parka and headed across to the cabin. The dogs had finished their meal and were once again curled in the snow.

"Where'd Paul go?" he muttered to himself. In the cabin, Billy dug into the cooler. "Funny," he murmured. "I was sure we put two packages of hot dogs in here."

He set the food on the bed so he could close the cooler, and frowned. This morning there'd been a sleeping bag on each bunk, but now this one had none. Was anything else missing? Yes, Paul's duffel bag. The saw still hung on the wall, but the hatchet was gone.

Billy ran out of the cabin and around the end of the mess hall. The snowmobile was gone too!

From the half-moon's bend the late sun threw spruce shadow spears across the lake toward Billy. Between the shafts of shade their ski and snowmachine trails stood out in sharp relief. Which ones had Paul made?

The snow on the nearer end of the lake, to his left, was still unmarked. He squinted against the sun to search the part of the lake visible from where he stood, and the white slash going up the hill. Nothing moved. He strained to hear the sound of the motor but heard only Uncle Jess's hammer in the mess hall.

What had Paul mumbled earlier, when they talked about living in the bush? "I go home?" Where home was, Billy had no idea, but he knew the Yukon River was a long way off. What if the snowmobile should

20

break down somewhere out there in the wilderness, or run out of gas? A guy could freeze to death out there!

Billy hurried to where the dogs were tied. "Come on, Molly. He's got a head start, but we'd better try to track him." He fastened his ski bindings and whistled to her.

He turned Molly first toward the road where they'd struck the lake that morning, but was soon satisfied that there was only one set of tracks, the one they'd made coming in.

"Ho, Molly!"

They turned again, angling out toward the middle of the lake. They crossed their old ski marks, then the big ovals Paul had made with the snowmobile, and his own ski trail going around the hump and back. There it was, the broad track of the snowmachine again, crossing his trail and swinging out around the hump. *The cracking ice!*

Around the hump he flew behind Molly, into the long shadow of the hill. The track led straight toward the slash on the hill. Ahead, not far from the safety of the shore, he saw the snowmachine. Its nose tilted into the air; the rear of the tracks dipped almost out of sight.

He gasped with relief. Paul stood near the machine.

Now Billy knew for sure why Molly had earlier veered away from the area of slumping snow. She had sensed that the ice underneath was weak. Shadowed by the hill, the lake's surface all looked the same now. There'd been nothing to warn Paul. Was the machine sinking? He could be in terrible danger.

Billy swung the dog wide of the area. He skied

21

along the edge of the lake until they neared Paul. Black water lapped halfway up the tracks under the back end of the machine. It teetered on the edge of a hole in the ice.

"Paul, are you okay?" Billy called shakily.

"I okay. Machine okay, too, if ice don't break more." Paul had trimmed some spruce poles with the hatchet he'd taken from the cabin and was trying to wedge them under the back of the snowmachine. One mistake and the machine could go crashing to the bottom of the lake, taking Paul with it.

Billy's stomach knotted. Why hadn't he stopped to tell his uncle where he was going?

He kicked off the skis and made himself move out onto the ice. He looked at Paul's longest pole, about

22

twelve feet long and four inches thick, then at Molly and the rope still attached to her harness.

Paul seemed to read his mind. He held out his mittened hand. Billy cautiously led Molly forward until he could toss Paul the end of her rope.

Paul tied it to the front of the snowmachine. Molly whimpered. The ice creaked as Paul stepped carefully around the sled. Yellow-brown water percolated up through his footprints in the snow.

"If we put that long pole across the machine, behind the firewall," Billy called, "we could push on each end. If Molly pulls at the same time, maybe we can move it forward."

Paul shoved the pole through the space between the seat and the front part of the machine. As Billy approached his end of the pole, a muffled crack sounded beneath his feet. "Help us, Lord," he silently prayed. Aloud he said, "Let's push together. Go, Molly! One, two, three, push!"

Molly lunged against the rope. Both boys shoved with all their might against the pole. Billy felt the front of the machine tip forward and settle onto the snow as it moved ahead six inches. The ice at the edge of the hole crumbled into the water.

"Go! Go!" yelled Paul. Molly's muscles rippled. Billy gritted his teeth and strained against the pole. The snowmachine moved inch-by-inch across the snow. Another crack snaked through the ice. Water seeping through turned the snow to slush. He tried to ignore the icy rivulets running over his boot tops.

"Help Molly pull," shouted Paul. Tossing the pole aside, he leaned over to start the engine, eased onto

23

the seat, and slowly let out the throttle. While Billy and Molly ran ahead, he steered onto the lakeshore.

Sweating and shivering at the same time, Billy turned to look at the hole in the churned-up snow. Wisps of steam rose from its surface.

Relief surged through him, followed by anger at Paul for putting them both in danger.

"Where were you going?" he growled.

Paul didn't answer.

"Why did you steal my uncle's snowmobile?"

"No steal. I have money. Fill it with gas and leave with friend to take back. Maybe friend let me drive dog team to Kuliknik."

"Your friend lives over this hill?"

"South . . . many miles."

"Even if you found your friend, how could you get to your village by yourself?"

Paul looked close to tears. "I think I find."

Billy's anger disappeared like the steam rising over the hole in the ice. "Even if you could get back to Kuliknik, what would you do then?" His wet feet felt painfully cold all of a sudden. "C'mon," he suggested. "Let's go back to the camp and warm up."

"You tell?"

"About the snowmobile? No, if you promise you won't try this again."

Paul thought it over. "I stay," he said. "Come on. Both ride."

Billy got on behind, clutching the skis and Paul's duffel bag across his lap. Molly followed as the machine roared out onto the solid ice farther down the lake.

By the time the boys reached camp, Billy's feet felt

24

like blocks of wood. He stumbled up the trail behind Paul to the cabin.

"I've n-never been so c-c-cold," he chattered as he shoved more firewood into the barrel stove, then pulled a chair up close. Taking off his boots he peeled the frozen socks from his numb feet. The warm air stabbed like knives.

Paul took his boots off too. He cupped his toes in his hands. "Warm feet slow," he said. "Hurt worse if warm too fast."

Billy copied Paul. "My toes feel like ice cubes. What would have happened to us if we'd got wet all over?"

Busy with trying to warm his feet, Billy didn't see the shamed look on Paul's face. The boy didn't answer.

His lack of response irritated Billy. He only wanted to make conversation. What's more, the guy hadn't even said thank you for helping him out of his predicament.

After a while the pins and needles stabbed less sharply. Billy limped over to the duffel bag on his bunk to pull out a pair of heavy socks and the moosehide mukluks Uncle Jess had insisted he bring. Thick felt insoles in the bottoms of the skin boots served as insulation. The Indians and Eskimos once used dried grass, Uncle Jess said. He slipped them on and wrapped the thongs around the legs of the mukluks, tying them snugly above his ankles. For a moment he admired the intricate beaded design that circled their tops.

He picked up the cooler with their supper in it. "I'll take this over to the mess hall." Without looking back, he left the cabin. If Paul couldn't be bothered to talk, why should he worry about waiting for him?

As Billy tumbled into his sleeping bag later that

25

evening he was still uncomfortable about Paul. "I'm so tired, Lord," he whispered. "I just want to ask You to help me with Paul. He doesn't like me much. How can I be friendly and tell him about You if he doesn't want to be friends? Give me the words to say and send Your Holy Spirit to work faith in His heart." The burning in his toes reminded him of the afternoon's close call. "Anyway, thanks for helping us out on the lake. In Jesus' name. Amen."

Late that night, Billy woke. Soft snores came from Uncle Jess's bunk. A log popped in the damped-down barrel stove.

Even though the luminous dial of his watch read midnight, the room was not really dark. Moon must be out, he thought sleepily. He raised his head to look toward the windows. A dark shape hunched beside one of them. Paul. Was he still thinking of running away?

Billy slipped out of his sleeping bag and tiptoed over to the other boy. He followed Paul's gaze.

Curtains of light hung in the sky, swaying, rippling, fading then brightening; yellow, white, greenish . . . moving in time to music he couldn't hear. Billy gasped. "What is it?"

"Northern lights."

This looked nothing like the drawings of the aurora borealis he'd done when his class studied Alaska.

The glow in the sky paled to let some of the brighter stars shine through. Suddenly brilliant arcs of light shot from one side of the heavens to the other, only to be replaced by more sheets of light rippling at incredible speed from horizon to horizon.

The light reflecting off the snow showed the dogs curled with their tails over their faces, sound asleep. Something moved. Billy nudged Paul and pointed. A big white snowshoe hare hopped out of the brush. Now several smaller shapes scampered out of the shadows, chasing each other around the bigger one.

One of the sled dogs raised his head. Suddenly the hares were gone. Billy blinked.

"Still there," whispered Paul. "Watch." Sure enough, when the dog curled up again, lumps of snow suddenly unfroze and hopped back into the brush.

The curtains of light in the sky swayed more slowly, fading again. "My mother say northern lights are the sky children playing."

Billy thought about that. "My mother used to tell me stories too," he whispered back. "She died three years ago. I still miss her lots." He watched the fading lights. "Aunt Adele and Uncle Alan and my cousins are family for me and my dad now. Just like Uncle Jess and his family want to be family for you."

"I too dumb for their family. Better off in the village."

"You're not dumb. Look how you fixed the snowmachine! Paul, give Uncle Jess a chance. And me too. I want to be your friend." Billy didn't know until he said the words how much he really meant it.

Paul studied his face in the dimness. Then Billy saw a flash of white teeth. Paul was smiling. "You not dumb either. I glad you came to help me on lake." He tiptoed back and climbed to the upper bunk.

27

Billy took one last look out the window. The northern lights had disappeared. Millions of stars pricked the velvet sky. They even sparkled on the snow-covered trees climbing the slope beyond the cabin.

Suddenly one of the sparkles moved. It flared, then flickered out. Was someone out there among the trees? Maybe he should tell Paul. He watched closely but the light didn't come back. No, in this land of surprises there was probably a perfectly logical explanation. Paul had just said he wasn't dumb. Let him think that. Billy decided he'd keep his mouth shut.

Mystery at Camp

As daylight streamed through the cabin windows next morning, Billy awoke to the sound of raucous croaks and squawks. Uncle Jess knelt, stirring the coals inside the barrel stove. He grinned at Billy's startled expression.

"Just ravens teasing the dogs." He shoved chunks of wood into the stove and shut the door.

From the window, Billy watched two shaggy black birds flap to the snow just out of reach of the dogs. They hopped as close as they dared, heavy beaks parted in guttural clucks. Billy laughed at the dogs' attempts to ignore the ungainly creatures.

"Billy, what's this?" Uncle Jess' voice, suddenly serious, brought Billy's attention back to the stove. He pointed to the boys' drying socks and boots. "I wondered why you were wearing your mukluks last night. How did you get your feet wet?"

Paul sat up in his bunk. Billy saw that the other boy held his breath. How could he answer and not get Paul in trouble?

"I . . . we . . . should have told you last night, but everything turned out all right. We took the snowmachine out on the lake. There's a place where the ice is thin, and it . . . ah . . . broke through." Billy hurried on. "We got it out. It's not hurt."

No one spoke for a long minute.

"I'm not worried about the snowmachine, though you shouldn't have used it without permission. But you boys might have drowned," said Jess. "Are you sure you're okay? Let me see your feet, both of you."

Billy's feet looked red, and still felt itchy, but were otherwise all right. Paul thrust his brown toes over the edge of the bunk.

"You both seem to be fine, fortunately. Wet feet can freeze in no time at all. Paul, I'm sure you know that. You're both lucky the weather's been fairly mild."

Mild? Billy thought. If this is mild weather I'd hate to be here when it's cold!

"I forgot to warn you about the warm spring beneath the other end of the lake," said Uncle Jess. He put one hand on his foster son's shoulder and gestured toward Billy. "We old-timers have to watch out for these cheechakos."

Paul let out his breath. His dark eyes studied the pastor's face uncertainly. "I watch out next time."

The morning passed quickly. The boys carried the usable lumber outdoors as they pried it from the dividing wall. They stacked it under the kitchen end of the building. Uncle Jess removed the row of studs. Then they rolled a coat of sunny yellow paint onto the walls of the new dining room.

30

"All done, boys?" boomed Uncle Jess. "Why don't you make some sandwiches, then you can take a break."

Billy dug through a box of supplies for the peanut butter and the squeeze bottle of honey. He opened a bag of potato chips. Paul spread peanut butter over four slices of bread while Billy drizzled honey over them and slapped on the second slice for each sandwich.

Leaving lunch for Uncle Jess on the counter, the boys scrambled out into the bright March sunshine. The dogs eyed the sandwiches clutched in the boy's mitts. Billy gave Devil plenty of room, but tossed Molly a bite as he passed.

He thought about last night's mysterious light—and about the camp committee's comment about intruders in the cabins. Could that light have anything to do with those visitors of two weeks earlier?

"Let's see what the campers' cabins look like," he suggested.

The boys pushed through the snow toward the first little building on the slope behind the manager's cabin. Large patches of snow had slid off its corrugated metal roof. The unpainted board cabin rested on posts, making the side windows too high to look through. Billy shoved snow off the steps with his boot so they could peer through a small window in the door.

"Not very cozy," he said.

The room was empty except for several rusty metal bunk bed frames and some sagging mattresses. "That all right," answered Paul. "People come here for camp, not live fancy."

The next cabin, built of logs, had a thick layer of snow on the old-fashioned sod roof. As the boys passed

31

the bushes that screened the building, Paul laid a warning hand on Billy's arm. The doorstep had been already brushed free of snow. A trail led from the cabin on up the hill.

"Snowshoe make," Paul whispered.

The boys crept to the door. Maybe the maker of that trail was in the cabin. What if he didn't want company?

Billy peeked through a window beside the door. He saw no one. Slowly he opened the door. Inside were the same rusty bunks as in the other cabin. Several cardboard boxes were pushed under one of the bunks.

"After we watched the Northern Lights last night, I saw a light up here, a flashlight, I think," Billy confided. "Why would someone come snooping around that late at night?"

"Don't know. Maybe it a trapper. Maybe poacher."

"You mean someone killing animals illegally?"

"Maybe."

Billy shoved at the boxes under the bunk. "They're heavy. Do you think we should see what's in them?"

"It all right to just look."

Billy tugged one out and pulled the interlocking flaps open.

"Old magazines," he said disgustedly. "Look at this—*Ladies' Circle, Good Housekeeping*—why would anybody keep magazines like this at a kids camp?"

He reclosed the flaps and pushed the box back under the bed.

"Whoever came here last night must have made that trail. Should we see where it goes?"

"Okay. We be careful though."

32

They walked easily on the snowshoe-packed trail, past more cabins scattered among the spruce trees. At the top of the hill they came upon a large irregular clearing. The snowshoe tracks disappeared into the forest beyond.

"Maybe we'd better tell my uncle before we follow any farther," Billy said. Paul nodded.

Billy wiped his nose and shoved his glasses into place. "This must be the ball field," he said, motioning toward a framework of two-by-fours holding up a chicken-wire backstop. "Do you know how to play baseball?"

"Everybody know baseball," Paul said, sounding offended.

"I just thought maybe kids play something else in the villages. . . ."

A hint of a grin brightened Paul's wide brown face. "That all right. We American too, you know." After a pause, he went on. "I need say thank-you. You not tell I took snowmachine, run away."

An answering smile lit Billy's face. "We're friends, okay? Beat you down the hill!"

Paul was off in a flash. Billy churned along behind, trying to stay in the trail. He packed a handful of snow as he ran to throw at Paul's retreating back, but the dry crystals exploded into a shower of icy bits as soon as the missile left his hand.

What funny country. Snow everywhere, but you couldn't make snowballs!

Back at camp, the boys told about the mysterious trail maker and the light Billy had seen. Uncle Jess listened closely.

33

"Probably just a squatter, glad for a rent-free place to stay," he said. "If so, we probably scared him away when we moved in, but we'll keep our eyes open anyway."

At supper that evening, the three of them looked with satisfaction at the work they'd done in the mess hall. New cabinets and countertops improved the kitchen. The boys had rolled a second coat of paint on the walls that afternoon. Now the odor of paint competed with the smell of spaghetti and toasted garlic bread.

"We'll put the boys and men in here to sleep tomorrow night. The girls can have the cabin we've been using," said Uncle Jess. The teen group from the Log Cabin Chapel planned to work on the building by the lake, Billy knew. They'd be here in the morning. He thought again of the girl with the mischievous smile.

"Who . . . How many are coming?" he asked.

"Four older teens signed up, plus Dave Perdue, the youth leader. A couple of the younger ones may come too. We'll do all we can tomorrow and the next morning, then head back to Fairbanks in time for you to do a little sightseeing before you fly home."

Billy wished Mike and Jodi could see the camp. "Do people swim in Half-Moon Lake?" he asked.

"Oh, yes. It's a little muddy, but the kids don't mind. Someday we'll haul in sand to spread on the bottom of the swimming area. We'll have a swimming hole nice as any Outside."

"Aren't most swimming holes outside?"

The others laughed. "Outside mean Lower Forty-eight . . . not in Alaska," said Paul.

34

Billy laughed too. *"Outside. Lower Forty-eight. Cheechako.* I need an Alaskan dictionary to know what people here are talking about."

Paul woke first next morning. He stopped lacing his boots to shake Billy. "Get up. We have time to ski before breakfast."

Billy pulled the sleeping bag up around his ears, but squinted one eye to peer out the window. Pink wisps of clouds against a pale blue morning convinced him to follow Paul's example. Within moments the boys headed toward the lake with Molly.

Buckling on the skis, Paul swept once around in a big oval, while Billy danced in place to get warm. Then he took a turn. His breath made little clouds in the frosty air. He felt much more at home on the skis today.

"Whew, that was ex-hil-erating!" He pulled to a stop at the foot of the trail. Then he cocked his head. "Listen. What's the matter with the dogs?"

The high-pitched wailing of Alaskan sled dogs rang out across the lake.

"Don't know. Maybe it whoever made the snowshoe tracks. I go see." Paul started up the trail with Molly straining against the rope to join her teammates. Billy shouldered the skis and hurried to catch up. Rounding the corner of the mess hall, the boys stopped short.

Two shaggy gray-brown shapes stood in the trail. Horses? No. A yearling moose and its mother. The calf was almost near enough to touch and looked bigger than a horse to Billy.

But the mother was even bigger, and mad besides. She stood between the leaping dogs and her baby, head down and hair on her neck standing straight up.

35

"Hurry . . . get under building." Paul grabbed Molly's muzzle to keep her quiet and pulled her over to the pilings supporting the mess hall. He wrapped her rope around a post.

Billy dropped the skis and scrambled after Paul, behind the canoes, as the two moose plunged past. Molly joined the sled-dog chorus.

The pastor rushed out of the cabin. "Boys, are you hurt?"

Billy and Paul crawled out from under the building.

"Thank God!" exclaimed Uncle Jess. "I didn't see you coming up the trail in time to warn you. There's nothing more dangerous than an angry mama moose."

Billy tried to stop shaking. "Wh-why did they come so close to the buildings?"

"This is probably their usual path to the willow brush down by the lake. They didn't know we were here until the dogs set up a fuss."

The three went into the mess hall for pancakes eaten in front of the fireplace. Despite the leaping flames, the room was still chilly. The pancakes cooled before they hit the plates, but they still tasted great after the morning's exercise. Uncle Jess forked one last bite, then reached inside his parka to pull out a small black book.

"Many people have met God at this old camp, primitive though it is," he said. "This week we're starting a new chapter in its history. I believe that God's given us a special privilege to be here right at the beginning. But we can do nothing without His help. I know He protected you boys this morning."

He was there when the snowmobile broke through, too, Billy thought.

Uncle Jess opened the Bible to Psalm 8. He read aloud in his deep voice:

O Lord, our Lord,
how majestic is your name in all the earth! . . .
When I consider your heavens,
the work of your fingers,
the moon and the stars,
which you have set in place,
what is man that you are mindful of him . . . ?

Billy remembered this morning's pink and blue sky and the northern lights last night. Out there alone in the middle of the lake, he'd felt so *small*.

37

Uncle Jess continued:

You made him ruler over the works of your hands;
you put everything under his feet:
all flocks and herds,
and the beasts of the field,
the birds of the air . . .

Even the fierce mother moose and the clownish
ravens!

O Lord, our Lord, how majestic is your name in all
the earth.

Billy thought about the beautiful words as the
flames crackled and sputtered. Gradually he became
aware of the sound of motors. Uncle Jess stepped to
the door: "Here come the kids."

Billy and Paul quickly cleared the breakfast
things, then jammed on mittens, caps, and scarves as
they hurried to the shore. Bursting from the forest onto
the lake came one, two, three snowmobiles. Each held
two riders and pulled a sled loaded high with supplies.
One sled carried three people.

The machines roared up to the landing. The new-
comers were bundled in puffy parkas or snowmachine
suits, their faces hidden behind breath-frosted scarves,
hoods, and caps. As the riders tumbled off the machines, Billy could see that some were tall, some short,
and all full of energy.

"Well, here we are. What do we do first?" called a
bearded young man.

"Dave Perdue, our youth director," said Uncle Jess. "Meet Billy Skarson. Some of the kids met him last night at the parsonage. And you know my right-hand man, Paul Moses."

Paul returned Dave's handshake uncertainly. Billy realized that the Indian boy felt nervous about the crowd of noisy kids now busy pulling bundles off the sleds.

"Up front, everybody!" Uncle Jess's big voice sounded over their shouts. "Just a few instructions. My dogs are tied up near the buildings. Most of them are friendly, but don't get too close.

"Young ladies will sleep in the cabin on the right. Boys will sleep in the mess hall. Carry your personal gear to those places and leave the building supplies here by the chapel. Then we'll have a short meeting in the mess hall before we go to work."

Paul had already disappeared with an armload of food. Billy grabbed a box marked "groceries."

Soon everybody gathered around the fireplace. Caps and scarves came off in the increasing warmth of the room, then parkas.

Billy saw that most of the kids were older than he—fifteen to seventeen. But one boy, Corky, looked to be about twelve. Little and skinny, he bounced from one place to another like a flea. Two other boys, James and Evanston, were Indian or part Indian. The two older girls, Irene and Helen, were twins, with shining straight dark hair and quiet faces.

The other girl, Susie Scalcucchi, was Billy's age. Small and pretty, with a strawberry-blond bob and merry brown eyes, she tossed her head and giggled at

39

a whisper from one of the boys, showing a glint of braces.

Billy stared. This *was* the girl who'd smiled at him at the Fairbanks parsonage. He came to himself in a rush as he heard his name.

"Billy Skarson . . . spending his spring vacation . . . And we want to thank each of you for coming to help us get the camp ready for summer," Uncle Jess was saying. "God's going to do some great things here, and you're part of it!

"A renewed camp needs a new name. Be thinking of ideas. Tomorrow we'll have a contest to choose the best.

"We'll work hard while we're working, and this evening we'll play. We found lots of snowshoes stored in a shed next to the chapel building . . . "

"Yea . . . snowshoe baseball!" someone yelled.

"That's right—and we'll have a snow cookout, and when it's dark, we'll come back here to the fire for music. But now, let's get to work!"

At the chapel building, somebody shoveled ashes out of a pot-bellied wood heater in the center of the room and built a fire. The older boys replaced broken window glass under Dave Perdue's direction. Then they stretched new screening over frames to keep out summer's mosquitoes.

The others hauled away an accumulation of broken chairs and other junk. The twin sisters swept down the walls and ceiling, preparing to paint, while Billy and Paul worked together to renail some rickety benches.

40

Susie plopped down on her knees beside Billy. "Can I help?"

"Sure. You can hold this brace steady while I nail."

Susie's shining hair swung close enough to tickle his nose. It smelled nice. She fluttered her eyelashes as she looked up at him, sort of like an actress on one of those dippy TV romances. Billy felt his cheeks grow hot.

"Do you like Washington state, Billy?"

"Uh . . . yeah. It's a great place to live."

"Do you ever go to Seattle? I was there once. I loved the skyscrapers and the shopping malls and the flowers and the boats on the water." Susie paused for breath. "If I had my choice, I'd live in a big city."

She sighed dramatically. "That would be so glamorous! Everything here is so *backward,* especially some of the people." She jerked her head toward Paul.

Paul, bringing another bench to be nailed, heard her remark. Billy saw the sparkle fade from Paul's eyes as he set the bench down and walked away without a word.

Just then the youngest newcomer, Corky, burst through the door with an armload of firewood. He tripped on the threshold. Wood flew across the room. One chunk smashed into the gallon can of paint the twins were stirring. Cream-colored latex splashed on wall, floor, and sisters.

In the confusion, Billy mumbled "Excuse me" to Susie, grabbed his parka, and hurried out the door after Paul.

41

Wild Man

Billy found Paul on the seat of Uncle Jess's snow-machine, staring off across the lake. He sat down on the one parked next to it. Susie had seemed so nice. How could she say something so unkind?

"I don't think Susie meant to hurt your feelings," Billy offered lamely.

"She just like everybody else. Think living in big city make them smart."

"But that's wrong. Being from a city doesn't help me know how to get along *here*. Everything is new for me. I feel really stupid sometimes."

"You soon learn what you have to know. But me . . . and other Indian . . . we have to learn too much new; what you learn since you were a baby. Susie right . . . Indian backward."

"No, she's not right!" Billy fumbled for the words he needed. "The Bible says we're all equal in God's sight. That means He thinks you're just as good as Susie or anybody else."

Paul continued to gaze across the lake. Then he turned to Billy and grinned. "You sound like preacher. Come on, we go nail more benches."

The boys started toward the plywood box of a chapel. The door burst open again, and Corky shot out, followed at a slower pace by Uncle Jess. Trailing Uncle Jess came Susie.

"Guess what, guys?" Corky shouted. "We get to go snowshoeing!"

Uncle Jess laughed at his exuberance. "It's a little more complicated than that. I thought maybe you boys would like to get the field ready for the ball game this afternoon." Corky bounded off toward the storage area under the chapel building. The pastor winked at Billy and Paul. "Corky and paint don't mix. This job should keep him out of trouble."

Susie smiled at Billy. "May I go too, Pastor Cassidy?"

"Oh . . . sure, Susie. Get another pair of snowshoes, Corky," he called.

Paul grimaced at Billy as Uncle Jess continued. "After you've packed down the baselines, why don't you collect a big pile of dead wood for the campfire? Looks like we might get some snow. A fire will feel good."

Snow? What did he mean? The sun was shining. Then Billy noticed a high haziness filtering the light. Off to either side of the sun were twin spots of brightness, like paler suns.

"Sun dogs," said Paul. "Mean weather will change."

Corky handed each of the others a pair of snowshoes, long oval frames of bent wood laced back and forth with rawhide. Billy clumsily tucked his pair under

43

his arm the way Paul did and followed the others up the slope. As they passed the mess hall, he remembered the saw Uncle Jess had used to cut the pantry shelving. He ducked inside after it. Maybe they could use it to cut wood for the fire.

Susie stopped to wait for him.

"Billy, are you mad at me?"

He blushed. "Why should I be mad at you?"

"I didn't mean anything bad about Paul. But lots of the natives *are* backward. My dad says they're backward and *lazy*."

Billy looked Susie in the eye. "Paul is my friend. He's not backward, and he's not lazy."

Susie looked unconvinced, but she gave in. "Okay. I'll take your word for it." She darted away. "Let's go. They're way ahead of us."

"These are sure small cabins," Billy heard Corky shout.

He and Susie caught up with the other two at the snow-covered meadow on top of the hill. Corky had already put his snowshoes on.

"I'll lay out the baselines," he yelled. He moved spraddle-legged over the snow to the backstop, out to where the pitcher's mound should be, back again to the chicken wire, and then out where the first base lay under the snow.

Billy watched Paul deftly slip his feet through the thongs and stand up on his snowshoes. He tried to do the same thing.

He took a step. Then another. He felt awkward. Suddenly his left snowshoe wouldn't move. He tried again to lift his foot but it seemed to have welded itself

44

to the ground. He looked down to see his right snowshoe on top of the left. He moved his legs farther apart and took another few steps. This wasn't easy!

"Hey, buddy," chuckled Paul. "You have wrong feet on!" Billy reversed the snowshoes. Ah, that was better.

Susie followed Corky around the baselines. Paul went next, widening the line with his snowshoes. Billy moved along carefully behind him, trying to keep his feet apart. He began to feel muscles he'd never noticed before.

"Where'll we have the campfire?" Corky wanted to know.

"How about over here, where the trail comes out?" suggested Billy. "That way we won't have to carry the food so far."

"I see some fallen trees over there." Susie pointed to the edge of the meadow beyond third base. The snowshoe trail the boys had discovered the day before led that way. They followed it to where it passed the downed cottonwoods.

Billy began to saw through a six-inch trunk. The others broke off dead branches to carry back to the wood pile. Billy sawed his tree into several four-foot lengths.

"Okay, somebody," he called. "Help me drag these big pieces back."

No one answered. He looked up to see Paul and Susie across the clearing, dumping their armloads. Corky had disappeared.

The sunlight had disappeared too, although the sun dogs still glimmered on either side of the bright spot that marked the sun.

Where could that pesky little kid have gone? Billy

45

moved over to the old snowshoe trail. Sure enough, he saw the marks of Corky's snowshoes. He kicked off his own. He could move faster without them. "I'm going to go find Corky before he loses himself," he yelled to Paul.

Billy started along the trail, moving as fast as he could. Occasionally he plunged through the crust, then stumbled back to firmer footing. The tracks followed a rough road cut straight through the birch and cottonwoods along the crest of the hill.

Suddenly Corky's tracks veered to the right, where the trail forked. Billy turned right, too, around dark-massed root systems of blown-down trees, and ran head on into a white-faced, shaking Corky.

"H-hurry, Billy. Back to the ball field . . . quick as you can!" Corky's wiry little figure on his big snowshoes scrambled past like an animated cartoon character. Billy didn't stop to see what had frightened him but hustled along behind. Maybe it was a grizzly.

Corky didn't stop until he reached Paul and Susie. Billy panted up in time to hear him gasping, ". . . a druggie, I think. He had a knife . . . wild eyes . . . Told me 'scram.' So I did!"

"You expect us to believe that?" scoffed Susie. "You and your big stories. You're always crying 'wolf.' You won't catch me this time."

"But it's true!" protested Corky. "I saw a huge, tall guy with hair down to his shoulders . . . a wild man, I tell you!"

Maybe he's not making this up, thought Billy. After all, someone was in the camper's cabin, and I myself saw that light last night.

"Why did you go off by yourself?" he asked.

46

"I just wanted to see where the trail went. The guy must have come from the other direction and turned at the fork ahead of me . . . or maybe he was watching us. He had a heavy pack on his back, and he acted mad when he saw me . . . real mad!"

"Huh!" Susie's expression showed her scorn.

"We could follow and see what he's up to," suggested Billy. "After all, Uncle Jess did say to let him know if we saw anything unusual. So he'd sort of given permission to investigate, hadn't he? Even if he's bad as Corky says, he couldn't do anything to four of us."

Susie still looked doubtful. Billy didn't feel brave at all once the suggestion was made, but Corky, bolder now with the others beside him, wanted to prove his story.

"Come on," he urged. "I'll show you where he was."

"I go first . . . I oldest," said Paul. "Take off snowshoe, go faster." They crowded close behind him. "Everyone be quiet . . ." he said sternly. "Don't want him to see us."

In the woods the snow seemed less deep. They could walk on the packed-down prints of the snowshoes. When they rounded the uprooted trees where Billy had met Corky, Paul signaled them again to stay silent.

The trail led between black spruce trees, lower branches weighted with snow. The four clustered together, holding their breaths while they crept around each bend. Billy realized that they were paralleling the edge of the ball field when he glimpsed an open area, and far across it, the chicken-wire backstop.

Now the trail meandered down through a grove of

47

birch. Tatters of "paper" fluttered from the dainty white trunks, stirred by the first breeze Billy had noticed since coming to Half-Moon Lake. The air seemed slightly warmer.

He slipped on an icy root and fell to his hands and knees. Behind him Corky stifled a giggle. Now they picked their way carefully down a steep slope which seemed to go on and on. Where was this "wild man" of Corky's?

The trees thinned as the trail dipped to a low brushy area. The kids crouched to keep their heads below the brush. Suddenly they came to the edge of a flat white lane . . . a frozen creek bed.

"We're on the other side of Half-Moon Lake," whispered Billy. "This creek must be the outlet . . . see, over

there's the chapel." They could hear the shouts and hammers of the others still at work.

The snowshoe marks crossed the creek and started up through more brush, into the spruce that grew on Half-Moon's "hump." Cautiously, they climbed higher. Suddenly Paul froze. With a quick gesture, he signaled the others to get down.

Billy peered past Paul's shoulder. Just ahead and below, hidden from the lake by the scrubby willows lining the edge, a tall, thin figure in ragged jeans and a camouflage parka hunched over, hiding something in the snow.

"See! What did I tell you!" stage-whispered Corky.

The figure jerked erect and whirled around. The kids flattened themselves against the snow, but immediately heard the crunch of snowshoes coming rapidly up the slope. Before they could scramble away, Corky's "wild man" loomed over them.

49

Baseball on Snowshoes

Billy's terrified gaze took in gaunt, high cheekbones and a thin nose. Black eyes glittered through a tangled mass of curly black hair, which hung to the shoulders of a ragged camouflage parka.

The man recognized Corky. His hand moved menacingly toward his pocket. "I thought I told you to clear out," he snarled.

No one dared to move. What if he had a gun in that pocket? "Help us, Lord," Billy whispered. Taking a deep breath, he stepped in front of Corky. The man's hand came to rest on the sheath of a big hunting knife at his waist.

"Mister, we don't mean to cause trouble," said Billy. "But this land belongs to the Log Cabin Chapel. We're here to help fix up the camp. You're trespassing, not us."

The man took a step backward. He glanced around, suddenly unsure of himself. "I'm just checking my trap line."

"What you trap?" questioned Paul.

The man hesitated. "Muskrats. I'm trapping musk-rats. I hide the traps in those willows along the shore." He scowled. "Now you kids beat it. Don't want no one messing with my trap line."

He turned back to his pack, slung it to his shoulder, and glared at the kids as they scrambled to leave. Just before they passed out of sight, Billy looked back. The man was digging in another place, still watching them.

The four didn't stop until they'd crossed the creek and were well up into the timber on the opposite hill-side. Susie spoke first. Her brown eyes were full of admiration. "Wow, Billy, you were brave, speaking up to that guy the way you did. I was sure he was going to hurt Corky!"

Color rushed back to Billy's face. "Wasn't anything," he mumbled, pleased. "We'd better tell the grown-ups about him. He sure acted peculiar."

"Susie, do you still think I was telling a wolf story?" Corky asked in an injured voice.

"I guess you weren't. But you have to admit you have told some pretty tall tales. You can't blame me for not believing you on that one."

Paul spoke: "If him trapper, why we not see traps?"

"You know what else seems funny?" asked Corky. "When I saw him the first time, his pack was so big and heavy he could hardly stand up straight. But he picked it up like it weighed nothing at all back there."

When they reached the ball field, Susie and Corky plunged past the tangle of fallen trees. Billy wanted to keep going too. But they had a job to finish. "Hey, grab a load of wood," called Billy, picking up his saw.

51

"Not me," answered Corky. "I want to get as far away from that weird character as possible."

"He not come after us," said Paul. "I think he want to stay far away from us too." He picked up an armload of cottonwood. Reluctantly Susie and Corky joined him.

"Let's get the fire all ready to light when we come back," suggested Billy. "But how can we do it so the melting snow won't put the fire out?"

"This way," said Paul. He slipped on a pair of snowshoes and tramped down the snow inside a circle. "Bring some birch bark," he said to Corky.

Corky went to a clump of big old birches nearby. He pulled off several handfuls of the tissue-thin tatters. Paul piled the paperlike scraps in the center of his packed circle. Starting with tiny twigs, then larger ones, he built a tepee over the birch bark. The others brought wood, until there was a sizable pyramid all ready for the match. Paul laid a square of larger lengths against its base.

"Now," he said, "we go."

Billy took one last look into the dark woods across the field. Nothing.

Corky and Susie needed no urging. Billy and Paul followed more slowly. As they came to the sod-roofed cabin where the intruder had been the day before, their eyes met. Without a word the two boys detoured to the cabin and cautiously opened the door. Still empty, but something seemed different. Paul pointed to the place where the boxes of magazines had been stored. They were gone!

"Do you suppose that wild man carried them off?" asked Billy.

"Maybe."

"That doesn't make sense. Why would he want old magazines? . . ." Billy's eyes grew round. Perhaps something was hidden *under* the magazines. But what?

Outside the mess hall, Uncle Jess tried to make sense of the disjointed story Corky and Susie were spilling out as Billy and Paul joined them. Palms held up, he scissored his hands in a stop gesture.

"You kids missed lunch. Come on in, all of you, and have a sandwich while I figure out what these two are talking about."

They each grabbed a tuna sandwich from the pile on the counter. Uncle Jess listened to the tale, from Billy's mysterious light on the hillside and the discovery that someone had used the campers' cabin, to their confrontation with Corky's wild man and the missing boxes.

"The man *could* have been a trapper," the pastor said. "Other ponds lie along the base of Spruce Hill. A trap line could circle past those and come out way back on Martin Road. I've seen the shacks out there where people live by doing odd jobs and enough trapping to keep groceries on the table."

"But if the man we saw was the one who'd been in the cabin, what could he have had in those boxes?" Billy wondered. "Where would he take them?"

"Maybe just personal belongings. He had no business staying in the cabin. When we got here, he probably decided he'd better move on."

Billy wasn't satisfied by this explanation. His uncle, too, looked thoughtful. "I doubt that he'll be back, but just in case, we'll tell everyone to stay close to the group."

He put the extra sandwiches in a plastic bag. "Listen, you four," Uncle Jess advised. "Let's not say any more than we have to about this. We've got work to finish, and we want everyone to have fun—which they won't if they're worrying about your mystery man."

The twins rinsed their paint brushes in a bucket of snow water. One of the boys added wood to the stove and turned the damper.

"We've done all we can do in here," said Dave Perdue, the youth leader. "But we'll have to feed the fire until the paint is dry. What do we do next?"

Billy looked around the inside of the chapel. The torn window screens were gone. The new paint glistened; the repaired benches sat in neat ranks in the clean-swept room. "It's . . . nice. But it's so bare. A chapel should look more . . . more . . . "

"Welcoming?" suggested one of the twins.

"If we had some cloth, we could make curtains," said Susie.

"Kuliknik mission had diamond-willow cross on the wall."

"Good idea, Paul! I saw a few diamond willows in the area we'll be clearing for the utility building. And Susie, somebody donated a pile of colored sheets to the camp. They're in the kitchen. Look around for needles and thread and scissors, and see what you can do," Uncle Jess directed.

"As for what's next, Dave," he continued. "I have

54

marked the area that must be cleared for the utility building. We can cut the larger brush and trees now, and finish later on when the snow melts."

Billy and Paul followed the men to a spot beyond the manager's cabin. The trees to be cut were marked with red plastic ribbons. Most were scrubby spruce, except for one little thicket of nondescript bare saplings, their twisted trunks covered with rough gray bark.

"This diamond willow," said Paul. "It ugly this way, but when bark off, very pretty." He pointed to a dent in a trunk where a small branch had once grown. "This a diamond."

Billy saw other hollows in the trunks. "These too?"

"Yes."

Billy picked up an ax. Paul pointed out two straight four-inch-thick sections of trunk. He cut the willows close to the ground, then chopped out the pieces Paul wanted.

"Now we peel bark."

Uncle Jess poured gasoline into a chain saw. "Paul, you have a jackknife, don't you? What about you, Billy? No? Here, use mine." He tossed it to Billy.

They carried their pieces of willow to the mess hall, where the girls had found sewing supplies. They'd already ripped a pair of gold-and-brown striped sheets into enough panels to curtain the chapel's four windows and were stitching hems by hand.

Paul showed Billy how to peel the bark from the willow, being careful not to gouge the thin white layer of cambium just below the bark. It did not come off easily. Billy whittled away, strip by strip, until he came

55

to the first diamond. The rich brown wood contrasted pleasingly with the creamy color around it.

"After most of bark off, we smooth with sandpaper." Paul took Billy's piece. "We can tie with rawhide, like this." He indicated with his hands how to lash the pieces together to make a cross.

The boys had peeled most of the bark when Uncle Jess poked his head in. "We've got the trees down and cut up for next summer's firewood," he said. "Why don't you people pack the stuff for our cookout and bring it to the ball field?"

"All right!" squealed Susie. "I'm tired of sewing."

Billy swept their pile of bark fragments into the fireplace. Someone added more logs so they'd come back to a warm building that evening. They put the food into a couple of knapsacks.

Susie picked up one of the packs. "Would you help me, Billy?" He held the pack while she wiggled herself into the shoulder harness. He grabbed the other pack. They started toward the hill together.

"What will you do if that wild man comes back, Billy? I know *I'm* not going to play the outfield. He could be there in the woods right now, watching us."

The same thing had occurred to Billy. But he tried to sound confident as he replied, "Don't worry. He's long gone."

As they came to the clearing at the top of the hill, something soft and cold tickled their noses. The snow was beginning! The others shouted and joked while they tried out the snowshoes.

"You guys did a fine job laying the fire," said Uncle Jess. "Want to light it now so we'll have good coals when

56

we're ready to eat?" He handed Billy a metal container of matches.

Billy took off his mittens. He licked a finger and held it up to see in which direction the breeze was blowing, as he'd learned last summer while camping with Jodi and Mike. Then, with his back toward the breeze, he knelt to strike the match, carefully working it through the sticks and twigs to the birch bark beneath. Paul watched. "Good. I told you, you not dumb."

The little flame caught and whooshed into a bright flare as the birch paper caught. The smallest twigs crackled, lifting the flames to the larger sticks. A few snowflakes sizzled into the fire. Paul laid on more and larger sticks.

"Come get in the game, boys. The fire will be fine now," called Uncle Jess.

One of the older boys, James, warmed up his pitching arm while Evanston waited at home plate. Corky and Susie stood in line behind him. The others played the bases or in the field. Uncle Jess doubled as catcher and umpire.

"We're playing work-up, Billy," he explained. "You and Paul find a spot out in the field."

Billy grabbed a pair of snowshoes and hurried along third base line. He put them on at the base, then plowed out into the unbroken snow of left field.

He heard the crack of the bat and looked over his shoulder to see a large softball, dyed red, arching toward him through the falling snow. He leaped to catch it but his snowshoes tangled, and he fell, dropping the ball.

He pawed through the snow until he glimpsed a

57

spot of red. Scooping up the ball and rising to his knees, he saw that Evanston had collided with first baseman Dave Perdue. Evanston picked himself up and windmilled toward second.

One of the twin sisters, her usually placid face lit with excitement, played second base. "Here! Throw it here!" Billy flung the ball directly into her mittened hands. Evanston dived for the base, but he was too late.

Evanston brushed himself off as everyone moved up one spot. Players changed positions much faster than in any game of work-up Billy had played before. It was difficult to catch fly balls on snowshoes, but snowshoes made base running slow, too. And even a red ball tended to get lost among the puffy flakes filling the air.

The players joked good-naturedly when Billy came to bat. He missed his first swing. "Strike one!" shouted Uncle Jess. Billy squinted through the dizzying flakes, trying to track the ball. This time he connected, sending it right over second base and far into the field. Corky and Dave Perdue scrambled after it, but by the time they found it, Billy'd galloped home safely, amid cheers.

Near the campfire, someone had spread a plastic garbage bag to hold hot dogs and rolls, potato chips, cookies, marshmallows, and cans of soda pop. "Time for a break," called the umpire.

Billy slipped off his snowshoes and propped them against the backstop. He grabbed a can of pop.

In moments everyone stood around the fire with bowed heads as Uncle Jess thanked God for the work accomplished that day and the fun and food. Billy joined in silently with "Thanks, God, for protecting us this afternoon." As the icy cola cooled his parched throat, he thought again of the angry young man. Was he really a muskrat trapper?

Billy finished his first hot dog and speared another to roast over the coals. Across the fire, Susie threw back her hood. Snow flakes dropped like crystal ornaments on her shining hair. She strung a row of five marshmallows on her stick and held them over the fire.

"Watch out, Susie, you'll get fat!" teased Corky. He and Paul squatted on either side of her with their own marshmallows.

"Little boys should be seen and not heard," she retorted.

Corky bristled at being called a little boy. "Maybe you're toasting them for your boyfriend."

Billy saw her glance across the fire at him and blush. She swatted at Corky, but he'd already dodged behind her; she lost her balance, and her marshmallows landed in the fire. As she fell, Paul jumped to get out of the way. His gooey marshmallow flew off its stick and dropped into her hair.

When Susie reached up to see what had hit her head, the melted interior of the marshmallow spurted onto her mitten and over more of her hair.

Her eyes sparked fire, but instead of blaming Corky, she lashed out at Paul. "Stupid Indian! Why don't you watch what you're doing!" Around the campfire, everyone suddenly got very quiet. Susie herself looked embarrassed, but she stubbornly refused to meet anyone's gaze. In the campfire her marshmallows flamed and turned to charcoal.

59

Captured

"Irene, Helen, would one of you take her down to the cabin and see what you can do to help?" Uncle Jess spoke quietly.

Susie stomped off down the hill. "I'll go," Helen said. She hurried after the angry girl. Billy stared, unbelieving. Susie'd done it again! What was the matter with her? Couldn't she think for herself? She was judging Paul unfairly, by stereotypes. He squirmed a bit as he remembered that he'd been quick to judge Paul himself.

None of the others said a word. Paul stared at his feet. "How about another round of work-up?" Dave's jovial question came out unnecessarily loud. With relief the group scattered over the field.

As the most recent batter, Billy took the last spot in the outfield. Paul positioned himself close by, not joining in the shouts and cheers that rang across the snowy meadow. Snowflakes fell thicker and wetter. An ordinary white ball would be lost among the giant flakes. They had to strain to see the red one. Corky popped a fly that came down short between first and second base. Players scrambled after it, yelling orders to each other.

In the outfield, Billy searched for a way to make up for Susie's outburst. Paul watched the fluffy crystals landing on his parka sleeve. He broke the awkward silence. "Snow like this fall only in spring—sometimes first snow in winter. Good for snowballs."

"All right! Let's have a snowball fight tomorrow!"

"Listen." Paul looked up, squinting into the sky to the west.

Billy heard a low droning from the direction of the lake. A small plane? Who would be flying in this kind of weather?

Evanston found the ball, and the next batter bunted. Corky chugged along toward second as the players again rushed the infield.

The drone grew louder, then changed in tone, slowed, and stopped. "I think it landed on the lake," Billy told Paul. Without a word, the boys backed toward the edge of the field. They slipped between the spruce trees until they reached the snowshoe trail. Excited cries of "You're out!" and "Move up!" told them that no one had missed them yet.

As they slid down the slope to the lake's outlet, Billy remembered his uncle's warning to stay with the group. He caught up with Paul. "Did that plane sound in trouble to you?" he whispered.

"No, engine sounded okay," Paul whispered back.

First a wild man . . . now a plane landing on the lake. "We'd better be careful," Billy whispered. "and get out of here quick if we see anything suspicious."

61

The boys slipped out of their snowshoes and left them stuck on end in the snow.

The newly fallen layer muffled the squeak of the old snow under their boots as they crept up the opposite slope and slipped from tree to tree. Out on the lake, the flakes fell thick. Had the plane landed without cracking up? Where was it?

The boys heard voices ahead. Paul silently pulled himself onto the roots of a clump of spruce growing above the trail. He helped Billy scramble up beside him. With caution they peered around the trunks. Billy whistled softly. Out on the ice, just beyond the willows lining the shore, sat a blue-and-silver Cessna 180, on skis, its nose swung round to point west. Beside it a stocky man dressed in an expensive fur parka and insulated pants gestured angrily at the unmistakable gaunt form of their wild man.

"I'm sorry, Mr. Paxton," the young man apologized. "How was I to know all these people would show up? I tried to get word to you . . . "

"You didn't try hard enough," snarled the pilot. "Get the stuff out here, and let's load it before someone comes snooping." He circled to the passenger side of the plane and opened the door.

The boys ducked. The wild man headed straight toward them! He vanished from sight behind the willows, coming out at the spot where they'd seen him earlier. With his hands, he dug away the snow.

Billy glanced at Paul with an "I thought so" look. Instead of a muskrat trap, a cardboard carton appeared, then another. The youth struggled to his feet

with them. The boys could see other cartons partially buried in the snow.

"Move it, Rolf; move it!" growled the pilot. He met the young man and hefted one of the boxes to his shoulder. The men shoved the boxes into the back of the plane.

They made trip after trip. While they were behind the plane, Billy whispered, "How do you suppose he ever got all those boxes out here? And what in the world would anyone want with that many old magazines?"

"Not magazines." Paul's voice was tense. "That man Bede Paxton . . . I see him before. He the one bring the whiskey my dad drink in Kuliknik."

"You mean . . . they've got whiskey in those boxes?"

"I think so. Our village voted not to have alcohol. Paxton know some people will buy anyway. Him smuggler. He the man cause my father to die!"

"We'd better get out of here before they see us." Billy jumped to his feet, but Paul grabbed his arm and pulled him down. The men were coming back.

"Hurry it up. Snow's so heavy I shouldn't risk taking off, but I can't stay here," growled the smuggler. "Lucky I got in without being heard."

Rolf lifted the last box out of the snow. "Mr. Paxton, I . . . won't be working for you after this job." He sounded scared. "You didn't tell me your 'freight' was illegal liquor. I can't afford another run-in with the law."

"Listen, kid. You're not backing out on me, you hear? I know you're on probation. Just one word from me to the cops, and you'll be sorry you ever tried. Now get that load out to the plane."

64

So—their wild man was not so ferocious after all. Billy craned his neck to see if they were leaving. As he did so, his foot slipped from the icy root on which he perched. He grabbed for Paul, who also lost his footing. Both boys tumbled onto the trail. Bede whirled. The carton he carried hit Rolf's box.

On hands and knees, Billy watched in fascination. As if in a slow-motion movie, both cartons burst open, scattering magazines and brown glass bottles. Two bottles smashed together in mid-air and shattered, spattering brown liquid in a swirl on the snow.

He saw the amazed faces of the two men as the boxes and their contents spilled to the ground. Still in slow motion Billy felt himself trying to scramble to his feet. But the men moved quickly. A rough hand grabbed his shoulder and whirled him around.

Paul fared no better. He kicked and struggled until Rolf got his arm behind his back and shoved him against Billy, who cringed under the furious glare of the smuggler.

A picture of Paul's father, lying dead in a snowbank, flashed into Billy's mind. Bede Paxton preyed on people who couldn't say no to alcohol.

Billy stiffened his body and jerked away. "You let us alone. You've got no right . . . "

"Shut up, brat!" Paxton lunged, digging fingers of steel into Billy's arm. His beady eyes searched the woods to be sure the boys were alone. "Give me that rope you've got around your waist," he snapped at Rolf. He grabbed Paul with the other hand, while Rolf loosened the cord which held his knife.

"Over here." The smuggler pulled the boys to a

65

birch tree. Quickly he bound Paul's hands behind him, looped the cord around the tree, and yanked it so tightly around Billy's wrists his hands went numb. The boys stood back-to-back, the tree between them.

Paxton straightened, breathing heavily. "Rolf Wagner, it's your fault these kids got curious. You decide how you're going to get rid of them." He jabbed his fist into Rolf's chest. "They can identify both of us." He spun around, scooping up most of the fallen whiskey bottles as he headed for the plane. "Get rid of the rest of this stuff while you're at it."

Rolf fumbled in the snow for the remaining bottles, looking distractedly from the boys toward the plane. Rolf—"Wolf." The youth reminded Billy of a skinny, cornered wolf.

Would Rolf kill them now, or leave them tied up to freeze to death? Billy tried to yell "help," but only a squeak came out of his mouth. Rolf jumped to his feet and strode toward the boys. His tangled black hair fell across his face as he stooped over them.

Billy forced himself to look into the thin, sallow face. Surprised, he saw that close up, Rolf looked more frightened than dangerous.

"Look, you guys, I don't want to hurt you. But I have to have time to get away myself." Rolf unwound Billy's scarf and tied it tightly around his mouth. He gagged Paul as well. Then he did something to the rope that tied them to the tree; Billy flexed his wrists and realized that the loops were not as tight as before.

"You'll get free before you freeze. I've got to get out of here before your friends come looking for you." Rolf glanced nervously toward where Paxton brushed the

66

snow from the Cessna's wings. Then he picked up his snowshoes and headed toward the creek.

For a moment, only the squeak of Rolf's hurrying footsteps could be heard. Then came a soft "plop" as a lump of snow fell from a branch and landed on Billy's cap. Suddenly the air filled with bits of dislodged snow.

A breeze had sprung up. Out on the lake, sheets of falling snow slanted to the west. Curses exploded as Bede realized he could not take off with the wind at his back. He slammed the door. The engine sputtered into a roar. The plane taxied toward the far end of the lake.

We've got to tell Uncle Jess! thought Billy. He twisted his hands. No way could he get them free of those loops. Maybe without the mittens—he grasped the tip of his right mitten with his left and pulled. The mitten dropped to the ground. He tugged his bare hand against the cord until the skin wore off. He felt the fiery sting of the cold air against the raw place. Needles of cold stabbed his unprotected fingers.

Suddenly he remembered the jackknife he'd shoved into his pocket when they stopped work on the diamond willow. Twisting sideways, he finally reached it. Clumsily, he got it open. He held the blade vertically against the cord, then moved his whole body up and down until the last fibers broke. One hand loose. He quickly freed the other, jerked the gag away from his mouth, then released Paul.

Did they dare cut across the lake? Paxton's Cessna had nearly reached the turn-around point. He'd soon be heading this way. He'd run them down if he caught them out in the open. And where had Rolf gone?

"There!" Paul pointed to the far side of the lake. Rolf had reached the outlet, but instead of heading up to the woods surrounding the meadow, he followed the shore of the lake.

"He must be after a snowmachine," said Billy. Just then the boys heard their names echoing across the lake. They also heard the plane's engine rev up to full power as Rolf faded into the trees. The dark shapes of the ball players came into sight.

"Over here . . . here!" Both boys rushed dancing and yelling onto the ice where the plane had sat.

The bulky shape of Uncle Jess waved back. He leaped onto a snowmachine. Dave Perdue yanked another to life.

"Stop him! Stop the plane!" yelled the boys, pointing to the Cessna skimming toward them. The men swung the machines directly into the path of the rushing plane.

Billy's heart pounded as he remembered Paxton's order to get rid of them. He wouldn't hesitate to run right over a snowmachine. The snow blew directly against the plane's windshield, but surely the pilot could see the machines racing at him. Would he stop?

Paxton must have realized that the snowmachines weren't going to get out of the way. Just before he reached the half-moon's hump, he swung to his right, throttling back, and steered behind the hump. The engine speed increased as he made the loop. He obviously intended to circle past the machines and take off before they could catch up.

Billy knew that in the gathering twilight and the falling snow, Paxton probably could not see the spot where Paul and the snowmachine had broken through two days before. The water would have refrozen, and the fresh snow would hide all traces.

Sure enough, there came a grinding, crunching noise of breaking ice. The plane's engine hiccuped and stopped. By this time, the boys had reached the end of the hump. As they rounded the point, Billy saw a sight he'd never forget.

The sleek blue-and-silver plane floated on its belly in a patch of shattered ice and black water. Its propeller had crumpled against a pushed-up ridge of snow.

Paxton pulled himself through a window, onto a wing of the plane. It tilted sharply under his weight, threatening to dump him into the water.

He looked toward the men and snowmachines. "Get me out of here," he whimpered.

"Don't let him get away, Uncle Jess," called Billy.

The two men swung their snowmachines far out on solid ice, crossing to the shore behind the plane. Billy saw Uncle Jess picking his way onto the ice. "Can't get too close," he called. "Dave, would you and the boys get some rope?"

"Hurry," whined the smuggler. "The plane is sinking!"

Billy couldn't help a feeling of satisfaction. Paxton was getting exactly what he deserved.

He and Paul crowded onto the machine behind Dave. They passed James, Evanston, and Corky heading out on the third machine to see the excitement.

"Be right back," said Dave. He ducked into the storage area beneath the chapel to look for a piece of rope.

"The girls are alone. We'd better see where Rolf

69

went," Billy said to Paul. Dave came out with the coil of rope. The boys jumped off the machine. "You go ahead, Dave. We'll tell the girls we're all right."

The machine roared off as the boys started up the path. Irene must have joined the other girls in their cabin. Nothing moved, except for the snow flakes, smaller and fewer now.

Suddenly there were vicious snarls from the direction of the mess hall, then a terrified yell. Billy heard shouts from Susie and the twins.

As he rounded the corner of the mess hall he sprawled across the dog sled. Who'd left that there? All of the dogs were leaping and howling, except for Devil. He stood snarling above a cowering Rolf.

A Night of Excitement

Rolf flung up an arm to fend off the snarling dog. Devil's jaws locked on the sleeve of the camouflage parka. Out of the corner of his eye, Billy saw Susie shrieking at the cabin door, while beside her the twins shouted at Devil to stop. Rolf's hoarse cries added to the bedlam.

Paul grabbed a piece of board and forced Devil back. Rolf rolled out of range of the dog's tether. Before he could scramble to his feet, Billy landed with a flying leap on his back, knocking him down again.

"Help me!" Billy shouted to the girls. "He's a smuggler, and he's trying to steal the dog sled."

But Billy's tackle had knocked all the fight, as well as the breath, from the skinny youth. Face in the snow, he lay with his right arm bent behind him, Billy straddling his back. Rolf raised his head to look at the blood soaking through his left parka sleeve, then at Paul, still gripping the chunk of two-by-four.

"I give up," he gasped. "I only wanted to get away from Paxton."

71

"His plane went through the ice." Billy tried to sound fierce. "My uncle is taking care of him, and he'll take care of you too, if you try anything funny."

"Let me up. I won't hurt you."

Rolf stumbled to his feet, hunching over his injured arm.

"I'll go tell the men," said Irene. "There's a first-aid kit in the kitchen. Maybe you should bandage his arm." She headed for the lake.

"C'mon." Billy led the way into the dim mess hall. Rolf collapsed onto a chair near the logs still smoldering in the fireplace, and gingerly removed his parka.

Susie darted into the kitchen and came back with the kit. She peered at the bloody arm and shuddered. "I'll get a wet cloth so you can wash it first."

Devil's fangs had punctured the knitted wristlet under the quilting of Rolf's parka sleeve, slashing the youth's forearm. Billy could see the cuts were not deep. He wiped away the blood, squeezed antiseptic salve over the wounds and wrapped gauze around the arm.

Rolf fingered the bandage. "Thanks. I . . . I'm sorry you guys had to get mixed up in this." He stood up, reaching for his parka.

Paul stepped in front of the door with his two-by-four. "Where you going?"

Rolf shifted his glance uncertainly from one boy to the other. "I'll walk back to my cabin now that the men have Paxton. I won't take your dog sled."

"No way." Billy motioned to the chair. "We're keeping you here 'til my uncle comes back." Paul nodded, scowling, and took a tighter grip on his two-by-four.

Rolf sat down. Billy threw wood on the fire. In a

72

few moments, flames leaped up to brighten the dim room.

Susie went to a window overlooking the lake. "Here they come," she announced. Billy peered out. In the twilight, he made out the three snowmachines coming single file around the point. Uncle Jess drove the first one, with the rescued pilot riding behind him.

Suddenly, the first machine veered off toward the far end of the lake. What was wrong? Snowmachines two and three swerved to follow. Billy saw Paxton wave them back. The machine carrying Uncle Jess and the pilot disappeared into the woods.

Within moments, Dave Perdue burst into the room, the older boys, Corky, and Irene right behind him. "Are

you kids all right?" He saw Rolf in the chair, Paul still standing guard. "Who's this guy? And what's going on out there? The pilot pulled a gun, . . . threatened to shoot if we followed!"

"Paul says the pilot is Bede Paxton," answered Billy. "He smuggles liquor to the villages. This is Rolf. What's your last name, Rolf?"

"Heinrich," mumbled the no-longer-wild man.

"Rolf carried the liquor out there for Paxton to pick up. He says he didn't want to, but Paxton wouldn't let him quit."

Dave looked sharply at the dejected youth sagging in the chair. "That so, Rolf?"

Rolf nodded. He straightened, tossing back his tangled mane, and fearfully looked at the youth leader. "Paxton hired me to help pack some 'freight' out here. I didn't know what he was up to at first; then I didn't know how to get out of it. He told me to meet him today to load the stuff on the plane, but neither of us knew you'd be here.

"I carried the boxes to the point at night, going the long way around so nobody would see me." He paused. "Bede Paxton knows I'm on probation—said he'd get me in trouble with the law if I backed out."

"Dave," Billy interrupted. "Someone's got to help Uncle Jess!"

"You're right. I'll try to follow, but Paxton has a gun. I don't dare get too close."

Dave turned to leave, then came back to Rolf. "If what you say is true, we'll go to bat for you. Can I trust you to stay here?"

Billy could see Rolf's struggle mirrored on his face.

"I . . . I'll stay. I promise."

"I'm on my way then. All of you . . ." Dave looked very solemn, "pray hard that I'll find Jess safe and that no one gets hurt."

The snowmachine headed across the lake. Billy found a kerosene lamp in the kitchen, searched for a match, and lit the wick. Replacing the smoky chimney, he carried the lamp to the fireplace. Susie was trying to explain what had happened over the babble of questions and exclamations. She gave up.

"You tell them, Billy," she said.

"Quiet down, everybody. Let him talk!" shouted someone.

Billy set the lamp on the mantle, then explained the smuggling scheme. "Rolf's okay. Paxton blackmailed him into helping. Now Paxton has taken Uncle—Pastor—Jess hostage. You heard Dave ask us to pray."

"Why don't we pray like we do at our regular meetings?" suggested Helen. The kids moved into a circle that included Paul, Rolf, and Billy. Someone took Billy's hand. He hesitated, then reached out for Rolf's.

Helen bowed her head. Billy ducked his, too, as she asked God to protect Dave and the pastor. Others prayed, then Billy took a deep breath and spoke out loud. "Lord, we came to work at this camp so more people can get to know You. Please don't let anything happen to spoil it now. Keep the men safe, and don't let Bede Paxton get away with hurting anyone else. And Lord, help Rolf to know You love him too. In Jesus name. Amen."

75

"Amen," several voices said. Billy looked up to see Rolf glancing around the group with a peculiar expression, as if he were trying not to cry.

Finally Irene broke the silence. "The men will be cold when they get back," she said. "Can we heat water for cocoa in the fireplace?"

"I show you," answered Paul. In the kitchen he found a bar of soap and rubbed it over the bottom and sides of the big metal coffeepot which sat on top of the cold cook stove. "Make soot easy to wash off."

Billy poured water from a big kettle into the coffeepot. Paul carried it over to the fireplace, setting it close to the flames. Some of the kids stood at the windows, peering out into the darkness. Even though Billy felt better after they prayed, he still felt a funny tightness in his throat, a jumpy feeling in the pit of his stomach. He needed to be doing something.

"Paul," he whispered, "let's walk out to meet the men." Paul nodded. Zipping up their parkas, they slipped out the door.

Overhead, stars peeked through rips in the cloud cover. The snow reflected enough light so they easily found the snowmachine trail across the lake. Billy pulled his scarf up over his cheeks and chin against the bite of the dropping temperature. Fresh snow packed under his boots when he stepped off the trail. Good snowballs tomorrow, if they should feel like making snowballs. Where *were* the men? Bede Paxton was desperate enough to kill Uncle Jess if he thought he had to.

Out on the lake, the stillness was nearly complete. The squeak-crunch of their footsteps, the breeze hissing

76

over the surface of the lake, were the only sounds.

They stopped to listen, then broke into a run. The snowmachines were returning! Soon a headlamp bobbed through the trees. Only one machine?

It dipped onto the frozen lake. Billy's knees went weak with relief. Uncle Jess rode the machine behind Dave Perdue.

Back in camp, the girls passed out cups of cocoa while the men told what had happened. "Paxton kept the gun in my back until we were about halfway to the highway," said Uncle Jess. "Then he pushed me off and drove away with my machine. He'll be nearly to Fairbanks by now."

"Doesn't he know we'll have the police looking for him?" asked Billy.

"He'll probably try to get to the airport to catch a plane out of state. There's no phone here, so we'll have to move fast to alert the troopers." Uncle Jess downed the last of his cocoa. "Billy, Paul, Rolf . . . you might be needed as witnesses, so you'll have to go, too.

"We'll take the dogs and sled, and one snowmachine. That leaves the other for the rest of you in case you have any problems. Dave, do you mind handling things here?"

"Not at all. We'll go ahead with tomorrow's program if you don't get back tonight."

"Good. Paul, will you help me harness the team? How's that arm, Rolf?"

"It's okay," replied Rolf.

"You and Billy get the sled ready then. No time to

77

waste. And everybody . . ." Pastor Jess paused to look around the group. "The boys told me you prayed. Thanks! Keep it up, will you?"

Paul left first, with the snowmachine.

The dogs plunged through the dark woods, happy to be doing what they loved most. Rolf sat as far from them as he could, at the back of the sled. Uncle Jess stood on the runners at the rear, but he jumped off to run behind whenever the trail climbed a hill.

Billy gripped the edges of the sled with all his might and leaned from side to side as it swung in one direction, then the other. "Oof!" A bump in the trail jarred the breath out of him.

Finally, the dogs swooped up one last hill and onto a well-packed trail along the highway. They turned left, toward the lights of Fairbanks glowing in the distance.

Here and there along the road, lights shone out from dwellings. After a mile or so, Uncle Jess yelled "Whoa!" He dropped the brake on the sled and asked Billy to hold the dogs.

"I know these folks. I'm going to ask if I can use their phone." Uncle Jess hurried down a driveway toward a cabin tucked in the trees. In a short time, he came out and jumped on the runners. Away they went.

"The troopers are putting out a bulletin for Paxton. They'll send someone to the airport, and others will watch the roads out of town."

"Where are we going now?" Billy yelled.

"We'll meet Paul at the parsonage—leave the dogs there and go on to the police station. They'll need your statements."

Behind him, Billy heard Rolf groan. He half turned. "What's the matter?"

"I can't go to the police station. If they find out I was involved, they'll put me back in jail."

"In jail? Why were you in jail?"

"I was broke. Some guy talked me into dealing drugs for him . . . I got caught right away. They let me out on probation because it was a first offense. But I'd already spent a week locked up. I can't go back!"

Billy felt the older boy shaking. "You heard my Uncle Jess. We'll all stick up for you. Don't worry." He hoped his words were convincing. He had no idea whether or not Rolf was right.

Nobody Crosses Bede Paxton

At the almost-deserted police station, the boys sat down on a bench. Pastor Jess spoke to someone at the end of the hall. He came back to join them. "Well, good news, boys! They've picked him up already—at the Alaska Airlines ticket counter. In another half hour, Paxton would have been on his way south."

They settled down to wait for the arresting officers to arrive with their prisoner. Paul's face showed no expression. What was he thinking? Billy wondered. Rolf fidgeted. Maybe talking would ease the tension. "Back at the camp, Rolf, you said you would walk to your place. Where do you live?"

"In a cabin near Spruce Hill, next lake over from Half-Moon. I really do trap muskrats."

"Do you live there by yourself?"

"Now I do. I had a partner, but he left."

"Where are your parents, son?" asked Uncle Jess.

"Mom's in Anchorage. Don't know where Pop is."

"Does your mother know where you are?"

Rolf tried to sound as if it didn't matter. "She don't care. Told me to get out a long time ago. She's got a bunch of little kids to take care of . . . no money or time for me."

Billy looked from Rolf to Paul. Both of them . . . alone. Again he felt a surge of gratitude for the Marsh family—and his dad. And Uncle Jess.

Just then a blast of cold air billowed across the floor as the outside doors opened. Several uniformed troopers came in, escorting a glowering Bede Paxton. Though his hands were cuffed behind him, he lunged toward the boys.

Beady eyes glittered as he brought his swarthy face close to Billy's. "You brats think you're really somethin', don't you? Just remember, nobody crosses Bede Paxton and gets away with it." He swung toward Rolf. "Hear that, kid? Nobody!"

The arresting officers hustled Paxton down a hall and out of sight. A trooper escorted the boys and Uncle Jess into a smaller room, where the first two officers were making out their report. A balding, stern-faced officer shuffled through some forms on his desk. Pursing his lips, he skimmed over a handwritten page on top of the forms. Then he tucked in his chin, looking over the top of his glasses at the boys.

"Says here Mr. Paxton is accused of liquor smuggling. You the people bringing the charges?"

"Y . . . yes sir," stammered Billy.

"Where's your evidence?"

Billy looked at the others, dismayed. By now the

81

boxes of whiskey were probably at the bottom of Half-Moon Lake, along with the plane.

"We'll tell you where to find it," answered Jess Cassidy. "Why don't we just tell you what happened? It's a rather complicated story."

Billy's head was throbbing by the time the officer finally finished his questions.

"Rolf may go, in your custody," said the trooper. "We'll press charges if you're willing to testify against Paxton," he said as he showed them to the door. "We can't keep him from bailing himself out of jail, unfortunately. Maybe we could keep him longer if you want to press assault charges."

"Assault? Because he tied us up and told Rolf to get rid of us?"

"Yes. Rolf's story about getting involved unintentionally may be true. However, he did not untie you. A good lawyer would point that out. We'd have to charge both of them."

Billy glanced at the young man. "But that's not fair. Rolf saved our lives. He loosened the rope so we could get away."

The officer shrugged. "If he agreed to testify against Paxton he'd probably not be charged."

"What about Paxton's threats to the kids when the officers brought him in?" Uncle Jess asked. "Also, he kidnaped *me* and stole my snowmachine."

"The troopers noted those things in their report. At the preliminary hearing, a judge will set the amount of bail. He'll take all that into account."

The pastor turned to the boys. "What about it,

82

guys? A court case isn't pleasant. Are you willing to testify?"

Paul spoke firmly. "My dad dead because of him. I will testify."

Rolf bowed his head. He looked absolutely miserable. "Bede will say I helped him. And it's true, even if I didn't want to. They'll put me in jail too."

Uncle Jess put both hands on the teenager's shoulders and said, "Look at me, Rolf. I'll do everything I can to clear you . . . I promise. But if you don't testify, Bede's going to blame you anyway."

Through the tangled hair falling over his eyes, Rolf studied the pastor's face. His Adam's apple bobbed as he gulped. He hesitated, then nodded yes.

"I'm willing to tell what happened," said Billy. "But I have to go back to Washington."

"We'll cross that bridge when we come to it," said his uncle. "All right, officer. We'll do all we can to help."

Outside, the cold night air cleared Billy's aching head, but his stomach still felt queer. Aunt Rena waited up for them in the parsonage kitchen. Soup simmered on the burner. A plate of sandwiches sat on the table. The boys wolfed down the food, while Jess filled his wife in on what had happened at the police station.

Billy pushed back his chair. Now his stomach felt just fine. He jumped at the sound of the cuckoo clock behind him.

"Ten o'clock, boys. Want to stay here tonight, or shall we go back to camp?"

Nothing sounded better right now than a warm

83

bed. But Billy didn't want to miss one minute of excitement at Half-Moon Lake.

"I vote for camp."

The others agreed. In a few minutes, everyone, bundled back in boots and parkas, was out at the kennels harnessing the dogs.

"Good thing we're on the outskirts of town," chuckled Uncle Jess over the noise of the dogs. "You'd think they hadn't run in weeks from all this racket!"

Billy held Molly's harness while Paul straightened the traces between two of the other dogs. He saw Paul give a tremendous yawn and stumble a little.

Uncle Jess saw the yawn too. "Paul, you're almost too tired to stay on your feet. Why don't you ride on the sled with Billy? Rolf can take the snowmachine back."

"You'd trust me with your machine after . . ." Rolf's jaw dropped.

"Why not? We're on the same side, aren't we?"

Rolf pulled the starter and coasted away toward the road. Paul and Billy settled themselves on the sled. Jess released the brake. "Go!" he called.

The lights of the city faded behind them. Billy tipped his head back. The sky looked like black velvet sprinkled with handfuls of diamond dust. The Milky Way flung itself like a swirl of angel hair across the center of the velvet dome. Uncountable jewels winked out of the glowing dust.

Billy recognized the three stars in Orion's belt and the Big Dipper. Big. Much bigger than it seemed in Washington, looking up through the trees in the Marsh's back yard.

"Where's the Little Dipper?" he asked Paul. "Oh,

I see it. The two stars that make the front of the Big Dipper point to its tail."

"That end star in the tail . . . that the North Star."

"Oh," said Billy politely.

Paul went on. "That North Star . . . it never move. If you lost, it always show where north is."

Now Billy remembered reading about that. He gazed up at the star. It wasn't very big. It certainly wasn't very bright for such an important star.

For a while they heard only the creaking of the sled and the rushing of air past their ears. Billy's glasses felt like ice where they touched his skin. He put them in his parka pocket. Now all stars blurred into one glowing mass.

God was smart to put one star right above the earth's north pole, thought Billy, so that all the others seem to circle about it as the earth turns. A guiding light. He chuckled. He was thinking in soap-opera titles. Then he thought of something else.

"Hey, Paul. If Paxton is put in prison, does that mean people in your village couldn't get any more alcohol?"

"Maybe. Maybe not. Always some people can find a way to break laws."

"Isn't there a policeman in the village?"

"Yes. He a village safety-patrol officer. Not really a policeman. He work with state troopers."

"But if Paxton goes to jail . . ."

Paul squirmed sideways so they could talk more easily. "Some people say . . . laws need teeth. Too easy for him to get out again. But even if he stay in jail, bootlegger in village get liquor someplace else."

"What's a bootlegger?"

"He—or she—live in village. Maybe old person, maybe somebody who doesn't even drink. Just want to sell to make money. Hard to do anything about it because everybody related somehow . . . maybe cousin, maybe uncle's wife."

"Do you know the bootlegger in your village?"

"Maybe."

To Billy this sounded unbelievable. Laws were supposed to protect people. If all this were a TV story, after they'd seen Bede Paxton safely arrested, the courts would take over. He'd be put in prison, and all the loose ends would be tied up nice and neat.

Paul gazed at the snowbanks flying past. He spoke in a low, toneless voice. "When I little boy, my family happy. Then mother die, and dad start to drink . . . not when we at trapping cabin, but when we come back to village. He not mean, though. He just fall down and sleep. But some families, both parents drunk all the time. Little kids left alone, no one take care. Lots of fighting. Some people shoot others when drunk. My friend . . . his mom kill herself. Alcohol is bad trouble for my people."

Paul's voice grew loud and angry. "I hate what liquor do to my people." He paused, then almost whispered. "Sometimes, I think I try to change things when I grow up, but what can Indian do? No money, not know how to live in white man's world. I think it no use. I probably end up like my dad."

Billy felt shaken. What could he say to Paul? He couldn't even imagine a life like his friend described. And yet, he knew there had to be an answer.

"Gee!" shouted Uncle Jess from the back of the sled. The two boys grabbed the side rails to keep their balance as the sled whipped sharply right and down the embankment. The roller-coaster drop left Billy's stomach floating free for a moment. Then they were into the dark forest, heading for Half-Moon Lake.

He tapped Paul on the shoulder, motioning him to turn around again. "Paul, you're wrong. You can be different if you want to be. God loves your people, too. He loves *you*. He loves you so much He sent Jesus to die for you, so you can live in heaven with Him."

Paul's eyes were dark pools of disbelief. "If God love my people, why He let these things happen?"

"I don't know," Billy answered. "But I know that He loves you. I know that He has a plan for each of us if we belong to Him. Paul, maybe He wants *you* to help your people."

The Indian boy didn't answer. He turned to face front. Billy's nose and cheeks felt numb, so he pulled his scarf higher. Glancing over his shoulder, he saw Uncle Jess grin approvingly, and raise his hand to make a circle of his gloved thumb and forefinger.

At the camp, the lights were out. The four of them entered the mess hall quietly. In the firelight, Billy saw long lumpy shapes where Dave and the other boys slept. They shed their boots and wraps by the door, and crawled into sleeping bags laid out near the fireplace.

Somebody piled more wood on the fire. Then sleep blotted out everything.

Gradually, Billy became aware of an ache in his

87

shoulders, a sore place on his hip. He rolled over, trying to escape the unyielding hardness beneath him, then realized where he was. He raised his head and blinked at a shaft of sunlight that fell across his sleeping bag. A pile of rolled up bags sat against the wall, where his boots, parka, and mittens still lay in a heap. Shouts and laughter sounded from far away; closer at hand someone rattled pans.

"Good morning, nephew!" boomed Uncle Jess from behind the kitchen pass-through, where he and Rolf were rattling pans. "How do you feel this morning?"

"Okay, I guess," mumbled Billy. "Where is everyone?"

"Down by the lake, having a snowball fight. Think you're awake enough to tell them breakfast is almost ready?"

"Bacon? Do I smell bacon?"

"And hotcakes, soon as people get here."

"Oh, boy!" Billy stooped to roll up his sleeping bag. He fastened his boots and went out the door, zipping his parka as he went.

Slipping and sliding, he hurried down the path to the lake. He ducked as a snowball whizzed over his head. "Breakfast!" he yelled.

No one paid attention. Paul and Corky pushed a huge snowball into place atop others to finish their fort. Near the dock, Billy glimpsed Susie crouched behind another fort, stacking a supply of missiles. Someone else scraped snow off the dock to make more.

Splat! A snowball thudded against Billy's chest. He dodged another and scooped up one of his own, but whoever'd attacked him was nowhere in sight.

"You're on our side, Billy!" yelled Susie from behind her fort. He scrambled behind the wall of snow. Susie's cheeks were rosy with exertion; melting snow sparkled in her bright hair. She gave him a welcoming smile and tossed him the snowball she'd just packed.

"Thanks," Billy mumbled. He remembered the melted marshmallow and the look on her face as she lashed out at Paul. He moved away from her and peeked around the end of the wall. Just then, with wild whoops, the other side let fly a barrage of snowballs.

Leaping up, Billy aimed for a knit cap just rising over the top of the other fort. The cap went flying as a surprised Corky let loose with two missiles in quick succession. Billy ducked the first, but caught the second on his shoulder.

Out of breath, the teams paused to gather more ammunition. The sound of metal against metal rang through the air. Looking up toward the mess hall, Billy saw Uncle Jess pounding the bottom of a cookpot with a large spoon. "Breakfast's ready!" he called.

"We'll get you later," Billy yelled after the other team, which was already on the run toward the mess hall. He brushed the snow from his parka and thumped his glasses against his sleeve to dislodge bits of snow stuck to the lenses. He started after them.

"Wait for me," called Susie. He slowed to a walk as she caught up. She smiled fetchingly. "You haven't been very friendly this morning, Billy. What's the matter?"

It was true. Suddenly, he felt miserable inside. She was the prettiest girl he knew, and nice . . . except . . .

89

He stopped walking and turned to face her. He swallowed hard. "Are you a Christian, Susie?"

She grinned. "Of course."

"Do you believe God loves everyone? Indians too?"

The grin faded. "Sure."

"Then, Susie," Billy struggled to make the words come out right. "I just don't understand how you can treat Paul the way you've treated him. He's not dumb, like you think. And he didn't have anything to do with the marshmallow in your hair."

Susie looked embarrassed. "I know."

She ran ahead of him up the path. Billy followed, feeling worse than he'd ever felt in his life. Susie liked him . . . he was sure of it. And now he'd spoiled that. But Paul was his friend. What was a person supposed to do?

The Evidence Saved

Rolf sat at the far corner of the table and shoveled in hotcakes as if he'd not eaten in days, while the easy chatter of the young people swirled around the room. Billy had lost count of how many he himself had put away.

"More hotcakes, anybody?" asked Uncle Jess.

"I'm full enough to bust!" Billy patted his stomach.

Corky belched. "Me, too!" He grinned at the twins' disapproving looks. "We ought to call this 'Camp Bellyache.'"

"How about 'Kwitcherbellyachin'?" Boos greeted Dave Perdue's suggestion.

The pastor set his platter down. "Seriously, everybody, you've all worked hard, so you get the honor of naming our camp. Let's hear your ideas . . . *sensible* ideas."

"How about 'Camp Good News'?"

"Half-Moon Camp."

"What about 'Midnight-Sun Bible Camp'?"

"I've got it!" Billy burst out. "Let's call it 'Aurora Borealis Bible Camp.' The aurora borealis lights up the dark night. This camp will bring light to people who are lost in the dark night of sin."

"I heard somewhere that 'Aurora' means 'dawn,' " said Susie. "It's a perfect name!" She said it with a smile that told Billy she wanted to be friends.

"The 'Borealis' part means 'northern,' " said Dave. "Northern Dawn."

"Aurora Borealis Bible Camp. That's a mouthful," commented Evanston.

"Could we call it Camp Aurora for short?"

"Good idea, Helen. I vote for Camp Aurora," Corky said. "Now, can we finish our snowball fight?"

"As soon as camp's in order. Any more suggestions or discussion?" Uncle Jess looked around the table. "Okay, then, Aurora Borealis Bible Camp it is. Camp Aurora for short. Let's do the cleanup chores first, then pack your personal stuff."

"Can we go take a look at the plane?" asked someone.

"We'd better stay away 'til the troopers arrive. They told us last night they'd be here sometime this morning."

At the mention of troopers, Rolf picked up his parka and edged toward the door. "I . . . I'd better be going now," he said.

Billy realized he was afraid. "If you run now, it will look bad," said Uncle Jess. "The police released you into *my* custody last night, remember? Stay with us."

Rolf tossed back his mane and looked at Uncle Jess

unbelievingly. "You want me to go back to town with you?"

"Sure. We've plenty of room."

Billy grabbed a push-broom. While he swept the mess-hall floor, a dozen questions chased through his head. What if the plane had frozen fast into the ice, or worse yet, sunk? Would he and Paul be believed without the liquor as evidence? Could Paxton really be stopped? Billy himself would soon be back in Washington, but would the smuggler try to come after Paul or Rolf?

Three or four campers bantered in the kitchen as Uncle Jess supervised cleanup. Billy heard another sound—a clattering roar that rapidly grew louder and closer. Paul stuck his head back into the room.

"Chopper coming!"

Billy grabbed his parka and mitts and hurried out. Sure enough, a large helicopter whirled low over the treetops. It flew out over the lake and circled back to descend in a cloud of blowing snow.

Two troopers jumped from the 'copter, ducking beneath its whirling rotor. The group of curious campers waited at the edge of the lake.

"Sergeants Blake and Han." The taller man thrust out his hand to Uncle Jess, who was closest. "You people certainly threw us a challenge."

A few minutes later, Billy, Paul, and the troopers hopped off two of the snowmachines at a safe distance from the scene of last night's mishap. Billy saw what Sergeant Blake meant. One wing and the back part of the plane had sunk beneath the surface. The other wing jutted into the air, the plane held from going completely

93

under by the propeller jammed into the ice. Most of the cabin was under water. Billy took a few steps forward. The ice creaked. Sergeant Blake grabbed his shoulder.

"Stay back. The tail is probably resting on the lake bottom, but if not, we could lose the whole thing."

"But . . . the evidence . . . "

"Don't worry. That plane's not about to fly away. We'll get the evidence." Sergeant Blake snapped photos of the scene, then tucked the camera inside his parka.

Back at the helicopter, Sergeant Han used the radio-phone to report to headquarters. Meanwhile, his partner interviewed Rolf. Billy tagged along while Rolf showed Sergeant Blake the cabin where he and Bede Paxton had stored liquor. The trooper took more pic-

tures, then asked Rolf to show how he had packed the boxes around the ball field to his hiding place at the other side of the lake. Billy demonstrated how Paxton had tied him and Paul to the tree, and how Rolf loosened the rope.

The broken whiskey bottles still lay in the snow. Sergeant Blake put the pieces into a canvas bag.

"Here's one Paxton missed." Billy dug an unbroken bottle out of the snow. That would be some help, but they really needed the plane's cargo. How would they get that plane out of the lake?

The pilot and his assistant, the loadmaster, waited with Trooper Han inside the helicopter.

"We hired this chopper because it's big enough to lift that Cessna with its cargo," Sergeant Blake told them. "Sergeant Han is a diver. He'll go into the lake and attach the lifting slings."

Sergeant Han tossed his parka down to his partner and slammed the door of the chopper.

"I'd like one of you to take me over there with a snowmachine in case there's a problem. The rest of you can watch from the point if you want to see how we do it," said Sergeant Blake.

Billy and the others hurried across the ice to the half-moon's hump and along the shore to a good viewing spot. The men on the snowmachine swung across the lake to the opposite shore, where they waited for the chopper to lift off and skim over the lake. It hovered above the downed plane.

An icy blast from the rotors hit the group watching

95

from the point. The helicopter's door opened. Two hooks dropped. From each hung a long, broad strap, with a shorter looped rope dangling from its free end. The loadmaster poked his head out.

Then a pair of swim fins and black rubber-clad legs swung over the doorsill. Sergeant Han, clinging to a rope, spun down toward the plane. He carried an oxygen tank on his back.

"He'll freeze!" Susie cried.

"He'll be okay in that survival suit," Dave Perdue told her. "But see, they brought his parka along on a snowmachine, if he needs it when he's done."

The helicopter rocked a bit as it sank closer to the ice. Would the downwash from its rotors dislodge the plane?

Trooper Han guided the slings to fall one on either side of the up-thrust wing of the Cessna. He disappeared behind the fuselage of the plane as the clattering chopper inched even lower. Billy held his breath. His uncle and Sergeant Blake dared not come too close.

Suddenly Trooper Han crashed up through the new ice on their side of the plane. He tugged, bringing up the end of the sling he'd towed under the plane. He flung the attached loop of rope over the dangling hook. The loadmaster reached down to haul up the sling and fastened it to the hook. The first sling was in place.

Again the diver disappeared, coming up through the ice on the back side of the sunken wing. He missed his first two tries at snagging the second hook. If the plane should slip away now it could trap him underneath. The chopper dipped a bit lower and on the third try the rope caught.

The diver gave a thumbs-up signal before he plunged back under the fuselage. Sergeant Blake tossed a rope toward the hole in the ice. Billy glimpsed the diver as he came up and grabbed the rope. The other men pulled him across the surface to ice strong enough to stand on.

Billy let his breath out. The hardest part was over. Would the rest of the plan work?

Slowly, the chopper rose. The tail of the plane broke free. Slowly, slowly, the entire plane lifted above the ice as the chopper turned toward camp.

The watchers raced to follow, but before they got there, the chopper had set the plane down, released the slings, and settled back to wait on the lake ice.

At last! The blue-and-silver plane sat firmly on solid ground, propeller askew. One wing drooped because of a bent strut and icicles grew where water drained from its insides. Trooper Blake opened the passenger door. He jumped back to avoid a cascade of water.

Billy saw a jumble of soaked cardboard boxes—the evidence that would lock Bede Paxton up for liquor smuggling.

"This plane won't fly again for a while. We'll haul it to Fairbanks with the chopper," said Sergeant Blake.

A short time later, the campers stood watching from the edge of Half-Moon Lake as the helicopter lifted off with Paxton's plane. It labored away towards Fairbanks like some strange bird of prey, dangling the crippled plane in its talons.

"Time for us to get back to Fairbanks too," said Dave Perdue. Everyone talked and laughed as they walked back to the mess hall. Ahead of Billy, Paul and Susie tramped side by side. Susie spoke earnestly.

Now and then Paul nodded. When they reached the corner of the building, Susie saw Billy and beckoned to him. Paul went on alone.

"Guess what, Billy? Paul's going to let me help him with his schoolwork. I told him if he works hard, he can probably catch up with his own class."

"You . . . help Paul?" stammered Billy. "Does he want you to?"

"Yes." Susie looked down at her boots. "I told him I was sorry for what I said. And I asked God to forgive me." Her cheeks grew rosier. "If you could stay, I know you would help Paul."

They stood in silence for a moment.

"Billy . . . if I wrote to you, would you write back?"

"Would I?" Billy felt happy enough to burst. "You bet!"

Chena Hot Springs

Billy stood on the snow brake to hold the dog sled in place while Paul harnessed Molly and snapped her traces to the lead.

With Uncle Jess and Rolf bringing up the rear, the snowmachine caravan roared across the lake and into the woods. The dogs howled and leaped against their traces in their eagerness to follow.

Paul ran back to jump on the runners while Billy hopped on the sled. "Go!" yelled Paul. The dogs plunged ahead. Around the mess hall they flew and out onto Half-Moon Lake. Billy twisted for a last look at Aurora Borealis Bible Camp. Wait until Mike and Jodi heard about the events of the past few days!

When they reached Fairbanks and the parsonage, Billy looked around but didn't see Uncle Jess's snowmachine. He waited while Paul chained Devil to his doghouse. Then he helped unhitch the other dogs and tied them to their shelters. The boys carried their duffel bags into the house.

"Aunt Rena, we're home!" Billy called. "Where's Uncle Jess?"

Aunt Rena looked up as the boys came into the kitchen. "He called a few minutes ago. He stopped at the clinic to get Rolf a tetanus shot . . . he didn't want to take chances with that dog bite." She spread another sandwich with tuna filling. "They'll be here soon. Meanwhile, if I know boys, you're hungry. Right, Paul?"

Paul grinned. "Right!"

They sat down to wait for the sandwiches now toasting in the electric frying pan. Billy told his aunt how the troopers had retrieved Paxton's plane from the lake.

"I wish I'd been there to see it!" she exclaimed. "You'll have to come visit us again, Billy. I don't know when we've had this much excitement!"

"Last night at the police station they asked me if I'd testify," he told her. "So I think I will come back. We've got to stop Bede Paxton from hurting any more people."

A short while later they heard a snowmachine pull up and stop outside the house. Uncle Jess tramped through the storm porch and into the kitchen. Rolf followed uncertainly.

Uncle Jess greeted his wife with a hug that picked her right up off the floor. "Ready for another adventure, everyone?" he boomed.

"Oh, Jess," Aunt Rena protested, laughing. "These boys have had enough adventure for a while. Come on, sit down, you two, and have a sandwich while they're still warm."

Uncle Jess shrugged off his parka and sat down at

the table across from Billy and Paul. Rolf hesitated, then did the same. Under his dirty camouflage parka, he wore an equally dirty flannel shirt. A grimy, once-white T-shirt showed through rips in the flannel. He demolished one sandwich before Uncle Jess had lifted his head from asking a silent blessing and then reached for another.

Aunt Rena took one look at the way Rolf devoured the sandwiches and went to the cupboard for a couple of jars of canned peaches. She set those and some bowls and spoons on the table, and put out a plate of cookies.

Billy bit into a cookie. "What kind of adventure, Uncle Jess?"

"Rolf's going to stay with us, but he'll want his belongings. We can take the van out to his place on Martin Road and then drive out Chena Hot Springs Road. I thought you might like to see that not everything in our part of Alaska is cold and frozen."

Aunt Rena nodded. "The Hot Springs would be fun for all the boys."

"Can't you come?" Uncle Jess asked her. "Oh, that's right. You've got that meeting tonight. Tell you what. Since it's already midafternoon, we'll plan to stay overnight at the springs and come back tomorrow in time to get Billy on his flight."

Paul rested his chin on his brown fists. "I wish you not go home," he said to Billy.

Billy remembered his first meeting with Paul, in this very room . . . only four days ago. He'd disliked him at first. But now it seemed as if they'd been friends forever. "I wish I could stay, too," he answered. "But we still have the rest of today and all of tomorrow."

101

Rolf finished his second big bowl of peaches and polished off the last cookie on the plate. He tossed the hair out of his eyes as he leaned back in his chair. "Thank you, Mrs. Cassidy," he said politely. "That was delicious."

Aunt Rena gave Rolf a quick hug as she collected the dirty dishes from the table. Billy caught the startled, pleased look on the teenager's face. Bet no one's hugged him for a long time, he thought.

"Well, if you guys have had enough to eat, grab your overnight gear. We might as well get on our way."

"Okay," answered Billy. " 'Bye, Aunt Rena. See you tomorrow."

"Good-bye, all of you. Have fun!"

A short while later, the three boys, with Uncle Jess at the wheel of the van, found themselves heading out the road that led to Camp Aurora. They passed the spot where the snowmobile trail took off to the camp.

A mile or so further Uncle Jess turned off the paved highway onto a narrow, snowpacked side road. A signpost said "Martin Road." Occasional clearings beside the road held dwellings; nice modern homes at first. These gave way to shanties surrounded by old cars and litter half-hidden under the snow.

The track narrowed. The van wheels spun when they slipped out of the ruts. Billy worried they might get stuck. Finally Rolf pointed to a trail that led into the brush. "Right here. There's a driveway where we can turn just around that next bend."

Uncle Jess managed to turn the van and came back to stop in the road beside Rolf's trail. "Let's hurry. We don't want to block the road for long."

102

They all hopped out and followed Rolf along the trail to a tiny, sway-backed log cabin. Cardboard replaced a broken pane in the one window. Rolf had stacked firewood beside the door, but Billy could see that there wasn't enough to last long.

"It's not very fancy," Rolf mumbled as he unlocked the door.

He'd not exaggerated. A rusty metal bed sat in one corner with a rumpled heap of blankets on it. Dirty dishes filled a dishpan on the rickety table. A sooty kerosene lantern sat there too.

Rolf grabbed some clothes off nails on the wall and dumped them into a duffel bag. He picked up a burlap sack from the floor. Billy heard the clink of metal. "My traps," Rolf explained. "That's about it. I can come back for the rest later." Billy looked around. The rest? The cabin was nearly empty! Paul didn't seem to think Rolf's manner of living strange, as far as Billy could tell. But Uncle Jess had a peculiar expression on his face.

Back on the main highway, they rolled along past old homesteads where farmers grew huge fields of potatoes in the summer; past new homes with snow-covered garden plots and greenhouses out back. "Planes bring us anything we want to eat now," Uncle Jess commented, "but people here still love to garden. Vegetables grow big and fast with our long hours of summer sunshine."

Gradually the homes became farther apart. The van rolled through long stretches of unbroken forest. Frozen streams meandered beside the road. Now and then they passed a snow-covered pond.

"I wonder what Bede Paxton's thinking now," Billy said.

"He's probably trying to figure how to get out," said Rolf with a shudder.

"Let's forget about Bede Paxton," said Uncle Jess. "He's going to have to answer for what he did, but he's safe in jail now."

Rolf looked unconvinced. In a way, Billy was glad to be going home. He wouldn't have to worry about Paxton until time for the trial.

Rabbits with brown and white coats, big feet, and short furry ears scurried away from the van. "Snowshoe hares," said Uncle Jess. "They're losing their white winter coats, see?"

Suddenly he pumped the brakes to stop for a moose in the middle of the road. She lowered her head and stood her ground while her yearling calf high-stepped out of the brushy ditch and wandered across the road. The cow stared at the van, then ambled after her calf. She stopped to strip the tender ends from some willow shrubs by the road, her rubbery lips curling delicately around the twigs.

Billy released his breath. "Wow! I thought she was going to charge us!"

"One time moose chase my dad and me up tree," said Paul. "Dogs bark and moose charge them. We get down and finally catch dogs."

"What happened to the moose?"

"Went away."

Now the highway stretched ahead between rolling hills. "Not far now, boys. Ready for your swim?"

"You're kidding!"

"No. Chena Hot Springs is a resort. There's an Olympic-size pool, open year round."

These Alaskans! But Billy could almost believe anything. After all, Uncle Jess kept telling him spring had come, despite the cold and snow. Maybe people here really did go swimming in this kind of weather.

At last the highway narrowed down to a one-lane drive. They crossed a wooden bridge. Ahead Billy saw a long, level field. Beside it stood a pole with a windsock at the top. A small plane sat on the field. They passed a shed with gas pumps and approached a low log building flanked by two rows of cabins. Uncle Jess drove up beside the larger building and parked.

Billy's amazed glance took in other large log buildings and a smaller one beside what looked like a big, steamy greenhouse made of glass jutting out into the center of the compound.

"Ah. The pool," said Rolf. Sure enough, through the glass Billy could see the heads of people bobbing in a rectangular green pool. Beyond the glassed-in enclosure, steam rose from a ditch of hot water snaking away across a meadow.

Behind all this rose high hills. One had a big clearing where people on skis zigzagged to the bottom of a chair lift.

"We'll have dinner here later." Uncle Jess gestured toward the building beside which they'd parked. "Right now, let's go rent some suits and hit that warm water!"

Outside the old log building attached to the one of glass, Billy glimpsed an odd-looking tree made from piled-up antlers of some kind. At the counter inside, an attendant searched through a pile of swimsuits to find

105

trunks for each of them. He handed them towels and pointed toward the dressing room. "Showers required before entering the pool," he said.

Billy piled his clothes and glasses into a locker and stepped under a shower. Ah, that water felt wonderful. He'd not had a shower since leaving Washington! He wondered how long it had been for Rolf. He heard Uncle Jess offer Rolf some shampoo and ask how his arm felt.

"Fine. It wasn't a deep bite. I don't think I need this bandage anymore."

Billy pulled his trunks on over his damp body. Snug, but they'd do. Paul, too, had his trunks on. "See you in the pool, guys," they called to the other two.

He and Paul stepped through a sliding glass door into the steamy, sulfur-and-chlorine smelling big room. All the way around, snow piled against the base of the glass walls. He could see icicles hanging from the corners of the roof outside. To their left he noticed a square pool in one corner, too small to swim in. A couple of people squatted along the walls in water up to their shoulders.

The Olympic-size pool filled the rest of the room, except for walkways along one side and the far end. Small children frolicked at the shallow end. At the other, people played keepaway with a big rubber ball.

Billy jumped off the side into warm water up to his neck. "This is great! Come on in, Paul."

"I no swim."

"We can stay in the shallow end."

Paul climbed down the steps and waded past the small children, while Billy splashed toward him.

Before long Paul had gained courage to hold on to

the edge and follow Billy into deeper water, where Billy showed him how to flutter kick. "Now try this, Paul." Billy showed him how to duck his face and breathe out under water.

Paul tried it, but came up sputtering. "Breathe out, not in!" Billy laughed. "Hey, finally! There's Uncle Jess and Rolf."

Uncle Jess waved, and gestured toward the smaller pool. Rolf wrapped his arms around his skinny white frame, shivering, and headed toward it. Billy saw that somewhere he'd found a rubber band to tie his long hair back in a pony tail.

"Let's try the other pool too," Billy suggested. He and Paul hauled themselves onto the tiled walkway and hurried to join the others.

A couple of jovial young men climbed out as they reached the small pool. One had a curly red beard. "Don't stay in there too long. You'll cook," he said.

Uncle Jess moved from the stairs where he'd been sitting, getting used to the water, to the other side of the pool. Standing, the water came only a little above his waist. "Those fellows flew here in that plane we saw on the airstrip," he said. Slowly he slid down, his back against the wall. "Come on in. This will cure what ails you."

Billy stepped onto the first step and hopped out again. "Wow! It's hot!"

Uncle Jess laughed. "I told you, not everything in Alaska is frozen this time of year. The water comes out of the ground hot like this. They let it cool some before running it into the big pool."

Billy lowered himself one step at a time to a sitting

position on the bottom step. The hot water reddened his skin and made it tingle. Paul waded over to Rolf and Jess as if it bothered him not at all.

Billy scooted up a couple of steps to cool off a bit. He glanced through the glass wall at this end of the building. Without his glasses, everything looked fuzzy, but he made out a large, irregular pond of open water steaming some distance beyond the adjoining log building. A dark hulking shape came around the corner of the building and stopped not three feet from the other side of the glass. Billy found himself face to face with a massive bull moose!

Second Thoughts

Steam puffed from the moose's nostrils. His velvety muzzle twitched and his bell, the flap of skin dangling beneath his jaw, twitched too. Velvet-covered appendages sprouted from the moose's forehead. Behind those, big ears flagged back and forth as the surprised moose returned Billy's stare.

"Look at the number of points on those antlers," whispered Uncle Jess. "That rack will reach six feet by summer, or I've missed my guess."

Suddenly Billy realized what he'd seen outside the dressing rooms a little while ago. That strange gray tree was made of piled-up moose antlers, their shovel-like scoops of bony material scalloped with hooks and points.

By now people in the larger pool had noticed the moose too. A small boy scrambled from the water and darted toward it across the slippery tile floor. With a snort, the moose lurched backward. Long legs working like pistons, he plunged past the pond and disappeared into the woods.

109

A short while later, Billy and Rolf clung to the edge of the larger pool, where fresh water entered through an opening in the side. The hot bubbles tickled their legs as the water burbled upward. Across the pool, Uncle Jess tried to teach Paul to float on his back.

Billy told Rolf about the cow moose and calf that had nearly run over him and Paul that first day at camp. "Yeah," answered Rolf. "I learned to keep an eye out for moose on my trap line. They like to use a trail that's already packed down."

"Do you enjoy trapping, Rolf?"

The older boy turned to walk his feet up the wall, until his knobby knees folded against his chest. "No, not really. I'd rather watch the animals, not kill them."

From Rolf's skinniness, and from what they'd seen at his cabin, Billy knew that he barely earned enough by trapping to keep himself alive. "What would you like to do instead?"

"Do?" Rolf considered. "Oh, I don't know. Carpentry, maybe. I helped a man build a room on a house once. I liked that."

"What about finishing high school?" The question came from Uncle Jess, who swam up behind the two.

Rolf shrugged. "That's not for me. Haven't got the time or money." He meant he had to work to support himself. That hardly seemed fair, thought Billy. School was supposed to be for everybody.

Paul came churning along the side of the pool. "This swimming hard work!" he exclaimed.

Billy ducked beneath the surface and came up behind Paul, grabbing an abandoned beach ball that floated nearby. He lobbed it into the space between the

110

other three, splashing water into their faces. "Let's play keepaway."

Now and then other people in the pool joined their game. Outside, the sun sank behind the western hills. After a while Uncle Jess asked, "Anyone hungry?"

"Me!" shouted Billy.

Paul gave him a playful shove. "You always hungry."

In the coffee shop of the lodge, they sat in chairs handmade from saplings, around an equally rustic table of varnished yellow wood. The hamburgers, when they came, were nearly plate-size. Separate dishes held huge orders of french fries.

"Save room for a piece of their wild blueberry pie," cautioned Uncle Jess.

Country music and shouts of laughter came from the barroom next to the coffee shop. The two young men that had left the hot pool as Billy climbed in came out of the bar and ordered pie and coffee. The red-bearded one gave Billy a friendly wave as they sat down at the counter.

The waitress brought Uncle Jess and the boys their pie, whipped cream in the bottom of the shell, topped with a berry filling. Delicious! Finally, almost too full to move, they followed Uncle Jess out to the cash register to pay the bill.

Glass-fronted shelving formed a partition between the entryway and a small lounge area behind the cash register. On the shelves Alaskan craft items were displayed: wilderness scenes painted on gold pans, birch bark baskets, jewelry. Billy felt in his back pocket to

111

see if he still had his money. He really should take something back to Mike and Jodi.

Finally he chose a cribbage game crafted from a piece of moose antler for Mike. For Jodi he picked out a small purse of tanned moose hide, with a wild-rose design beaded on the flap. He paid for them. While he waited for the cashier to wrap them in tissue and put them in a bag, the others looked through a display of post cards.

A few people sat in the easy chairs on the other side of the shelving. The two young men who owned the airplane on the landing strip carried their coffee in from the lunch counter.

Suddenly Billy heard a name that jerked him to attention. "Paxton? In jail? We wondered what was going on." The red-bearded pilot spoke. "We were just taking off from Fairbanks this morning when we saw the trooper's chopper coming in, carrying a plane with a crippled wing. Funniest-looking thing I ever saw. Said to Jim here I thought that looked like Bede Paxton's Cessna."

"Naw, don't really know the guy," Red-beard replied in answer to somebody's question. "But from what I hear he's a bad one to tangle with."

"He's mean all right," agreed someone else. "Smooth operator though. This isn't the first time the law's tried to pin him down."

"Yeah. He always finds a way out."

Billy glanced toward Rolf, on the other side of the partition. He seemed frozen to the spot. His eyes shifted from Paul to Billy to Uncle Jess.

"Come on guys, let's go," said Uncle Jess. They

112

stepped into the frosty night air and walked toward their cabin.

Billy looked up at the tall youth beside him. "Rolf, those men don't know anything. Don't worry about what they said."

"They're right," said Rolf. "Paxton *will* find a way out. And when he gets through with me, I'll wish I were dead."

Uncle Jess put a hand on Rolf's shoulder and turned to look squarely into his eyes. "Now that's enough of that sort of thinking," he said firmly. "Didn't I make it clear before that we're all in this together? Paxton is going to have to deal with me before he gets to any of you boys. Besides, we've got God on our side."

That's right, thought Billy. God can handle Bede Paxton. All the same, he felt glad he'd be safe in Bayside until time for the trial.

Back in Washington, the weeks and months dragged along, but finally June arrived. With the closing days of school came the summons for Billy to testify at Bede Paxton's trial.

Once again, he stared out the window as the jet descended toward Fairbanks International Airport. This time, the hills were green, not white. When the plane rolled to a stop, he followed the other passengers across the hot tarmac to the big glass doors of the airport.

The crowd jostled him. What if Uncle Jess forgets to meet me? he worried.

"There he is! Billy! Billy!" He caught a glimpse of

Susie's honey-colored hair, another of Paul's brown face. Then Uncle Jess pushed through the crowd to shake his hand. Everyone talked at once.

"Camp starts in four days. Can you stay long enough for the opening? I'm going to help with the little kids the first week," said Susie.

"Maybe. I have to stay until the trial is over."

"Already talked to your Washington family," boomed Uncle Jess. "You're staying as long as necessary."

Billy grinned. It felt great to be back. "Paul, how did your lessons go?"

"Susie's a good teacher. I can read sixth-grade books already, and Rolf helps me with math. I'll be in a special study program next fall.

"And," Paul smiled shyly, "Susie's been telling me how Jesus paid the price for our sins. You were right. God *does* love me. And I think He can use me to help my people."

Billy's mouth fell open. "That's great! And your English has sure improved! I *guess* Susie's a good teacher. Or you're a good learner."

Uncle Jess beamed as he swung Billy's suitcase into the big blue van with "Log Cabin Chapel" painted on its side.

"You're right on both counts. You never saw anyone work like this guy works."

The van pulled onto Airport Road.

"Where's Rolf?"

"At the camp," answered Jess. "He lived at the parsonage and went to the alternative high school so he could work half days. Right now, he's painting the new

115

utility building. We'll drive out there now to get him. He'll testify at the hearing tomorrow, along with you two boys."

The van turned off the highway onto a dirt road, down the steep dip Billy remembered from his dog sled ride last March. Now berry bushes bloomed among the trees. Wild roses and bluebells brightened open areas. They stopped to open a gate. Overhead a brand new sign read "Aurora Borealis Bible Camp." The words had an impressive sound. And he'd suggested the name!

As the van rounded a curve, Billy saw the manager's cabin, the mess hall, and a building that hadn't been there in March. A tall young man came out of the new building as they pulled up.

"Rolf, is that you?" Billy had to look twice at the smiling young man. Solid muscles rippled under his paint-stained shirt. A neat cap of black curls had replaced the wild mop he wore last March.

"Sure, it's me!" Rolf stuck out his hand. "You haven't changed much . . . a few more freckles maybe, and you're taller and thinner. But I'd know that red hair anywhere."

"I need to check with Rolf on a few last-minute things," said Jess. "Why don't you three look around?"

"Let's go to the lake!" Susie grabbed Billy's hand, dancing along in front of him and Paul.

When they passed the mess hall, he noticed a couple of shiny new canoes stored underneath. An L-shaped dock jutted into the rippling water of Half-Moon Lake. Many of its planks had been recently replaced. A family of ducks swam in and out of the reeds near the shore.

116

"I want to show you something." Paul opened the door of the chapel building. Inside, painted benches and chairs sat ready for the first chapel service. The girls' striped curtains added a cheerful note. And on the front wall, Paul and Billy's diamond-willow cross gleamed.

"I varnished the pieces and tied them together with rawhide. Like it?"

"Looks great. It's exactly right."

They walked the few steps to the lake, along the damp shoreline to the dock. The bottom of the lake looked muddy.

"Do people really swim here?" asked Billy.

"Some do," answered Susie. "Not me. There might be leeches in the mud." She shuddered. "Pastor Jess says someday they'll spread sand on the bottom to make it nicer for swimming."

"Why don't we see if we have time to take a canoe out?" suggested Paul.

"We have a telephone now, too," Susie said as they headed back toward the mess hall to check.

"I *thought* I heard a phone ring," Billy answered.

They rounded the corner of the mess hall just as Rolf stepped through the door. "Pastor Jess, a lawyer wants to talk to you."

Rolf jackknifed himself down to sit in the open doorway. He lifted a white face to the three young people. "Paxton's being released. No one in the village will testify against him. Now he'll come after me."

117

Kuliknik

"What do you mean, no one will testify?" Billy asked, indignant. "What about Paul and me? And, Rolf, *you* know what he was doing. What about the whiskey in the plane? Letting Paxton go is just not right."

"Of course, it isn't right." The pastor's usually merry eyes were sober. "But if they can't prove that he sold the liquor in the village, they can't hold him on smuggling charges. And either the villagers are afraid to testify, or they're protecting someone."

The burly man sat down beside Rolf. "Young man, don't worry about Bede Paxton. We'll do our best to see that he doesn't bother you. Our lawyers have agreed only to a postponement of the trial. We're going to pray about this. I'm sure God doesn't want us to let him keep on with his smuggling."

On the drive back to Fairbanks, Uncle Jess seemed deep in thought. Susie, though, chattered about all that had happened since Billy's last visit. "I think I liked helping Paul with his schoolwork best of all. His teacher says she's never seen anyone learn so much so fast."

The van turned down Susie's street. Billy spoke softly so the others wouldn't hear. "Thank you for your letters. My cousins teased me about writing to a girl, but I didn't care. Sometimes I got to thinking it was all a dream, and then another letter would come and everything that happened at camp was real again."

Susie giggled. "It wasn't a dream. I'm glad you're back, Billy."

"Me, too!"

Billy and Paul cleared the supper table and put the dishes into the dishwasher for Aunt Rena. Then they joined Uncle Jess in the backyard.

"Rena started all these little cabbage and cauliflower plants in her greenhouse. Once they're transplanted, the garden's finished, at least 'til the weeds start to grow."

"When will that be?" Billy asked.

"They're already growing. See this chickweed?" He pulled out some tiny green plants. "Our long hours of sunlight are great for gardens—and for weeds."

The boys carefully knocked the young plants out of their pots, depositing each in a hole with a little fertilizer and root-worm killer, then firming the soil gently around the stem.

One by one the plants went into the ground. Billy's back felt permanently crinked. He yawned and stretched.

"That's about it, guys. Thanks for your help." Uncle Jess got to his feet, slapping the dirt off his pant legs. The boys flopped down on the lawn. "I've been talking

119

to the Lord off and on all evening, and I think He's given me an idea."

Billy rolled over. "What kind of idea?"

"Paul, you remember the Reverend Black in Kuliknik, who arranged for you to come stay with us here in Fairbanks? He wants to send some of the village kids to Bible camp. Our church has collected money for a few camp scholarships. Taking the scholarships to the kids is a good excuse to have a bush pilot I know take me out to Kuliknik . . . I can make arrangements for the kids with Pastor Black. Maybe I can get some information while I'm there that will help our case."

"I know people there. I could help."

"Yes. You're right, Paul."

"Me, too. Could I go, too?" Billy asked eagerly.

"Let me check with my pilot friend. If we go, we'd have to be very careful not to appear nosy. We don't want the villagers to think we're interfering in their affairs."

Uncle Jess headed for the house. "I'll call my friend Dan right now. And you guys . . . better get to bed. Remember, it's two hours later for Billy than it is for us. It's midnight in Washington."

Next morning, Rolf stuck his head into the room where Billy lay in a sleeping bag next to Paul's bed. "Roll out, if you want to go flying! Pastor Jess says to tell you he'll be back to pick you up in half an hour."

Billy rubbed the sleep out of his eyes. His watch said seven o'clock, but the sun shone as brightly as if it were noontime.

"You're in the land of the Midnight Sun now," Rolf grinned. "It doesn't get dark at all this time of the year."

Billy finished his last piece of Aunt Rena's good French toast with wild berry jam just as the van pulled up outside.

"We have to hurry because the weather report is for clouds to close in this afternoon," Uncle Jess announced as they scrambled into the van. "Dan will meet us at the airfield."

A few minutes later, they walked across a grassy area where small planes of all colors and makes were parked. Uncle Jess led them toward a bright red Piper Cherokee. A blond young man in a baseball cap stepped up on a wing to open the door and move the front passenger seat ahead. The boys climbed into the back.

Uncle Jess hunched over to ease himself into the front passenger seat while Dan spun the propeller to start the engine. Dodging this way and that to miss other parked planes, they taxied toward the runway, then paused while the pilot spoke into his microphone. He looked both ways, and when the controller gave clearance, he revved up the engine to roll out onto the paved expanse.

The runway whizzed by. With a small bump, they lifted off toward the sky. Below, Billy saw a long narrow lake where float planes sat like mosquitoes in a row.

Dan turned to avoid the flight paths of the big jets on the opposite side of the airport and curved out over the broad gray Tanana River and back, heading for the hills north of the city. The plane bounced as warm air currents from cleared fields lifted it.

Billy tightened his seat belt. He stole a nervous

121

glance at Paul, who seemed not to notice the jouncing. The pilot and Jess laughed together over some joke. He relaxed a little and watched the hills come nearer as the plane continued to climb. Suddenly a hilltop loomed very close beneath them, feathery green with the new leaves of birch and willow on the south side. Stunted spruce ran down the north side.

They crossed a valley filled with curving heaps of broken rock. Paul pointed. "Gold dredge did that."

Then there were more and higher hills, dropping suddenly to flat country which stretched into the hazy distance. "Look, Paul. You can see where that river used to go," Billy said. Old loops of river bed looked like smooth green curves of ribbon, lying on either side of the silver line of a stream. As the plane skimmed lower, Billy saw that the green was not really smooth. Brush and reeds grew in the swampy loops. Here and there the stream had left behind a little lake.

"Watch those wet places. Might see moose."

Sure enough, in a moment the pilot banked the plane so Billy could see below them a bull moose standing knee-deep in a pond.

After many miles, the country changed as they neared a large river. They saw another moose in a patch of willow brush, then a black bear with two cubs.

Smooth sandbars followed the river's inside curves and sometimes rose above the water's surface. The plane dipped lower.

Paul's face broke into a grin. "We're almost there. That's Tom Gooden's fish trap." He pointed to what looked like a child's paddle-wheel toy slowly turning in the gray-brown water below. Beside it, a narrow flat-bottomed boat swung in the current. A man stood on a platform that was part of the trap.

"He's collecting fish from the box," said Uncle Jess. "As one basket dips into the river it catches any fish swimming through that place. As the second basket comes around and dips into the water, the first one comes up and drops the fish down a chute and into the box."

The Piper Cherokee skimmed along the river, very close to the treetops. Then it touched down and rolled along a narrow dirt strip. It stopped near a corrugated-metal building that served as the airport terminal.

As Billy stepped onto the wing of the plane, he saw a dirt lane leading toward some log cabins. A hand-painted sign said, "Welcome to Kuliknik."

A man came out of the metal building.

"Okay to leave the plane here?" Uncle Jess asked. "We're looking for the Reverend Black."

"Fine. I saw Black at the trading post a little while ago."

"Thanks, neighbor." Uncle Jess led the way toward the village.

They passed several small log houses. The door of one stood open to the sunshine. Rock music blared from inside.

In the yard of another house, a man with a bright rag tied around his head stirred something fishy-smelling in a big kettle over a fire. His face lit up with a gap-toothed grin when he recognized Paul. He pointed to several dogs tied behind his cabin.

"I'll catch up with you," Paul told Billy. He ran to

123

a big white dog, which had almost wagged itself into knots with excitement.

Billy and his uncle watched Paul's reunion with Koolaa. Then they stepped onto the porch of a large log building. Two dirty-faced little girls scuttled past them down the steps.

Billy heard voices inside. He glimpsed cases of soda pop stacked next to the door. An old refrigerator stood beside them. A glass counter held cartons of candy bars and bubble gum. One wall was lined with canned goods, boxes of potato chips, bags of sugar and flour.

The voices came from several men lounging around a small table. Pastor Black, a short, balding man with a fringe of curly white hair, greeted Uncle Jess enthusiastically.

Then he introduced them to the three Indian men with him. "Daniel and his son Matt are helping me with the work on the new church," he said. "Jackson here is our village safety-patrol officer."

Billy filed that bit of information. He listened for a while as the men talked, but soon his eyes wandered to the candy in the display case. Breakfast seemed a long time ago, and he still had the dollar he'd stuck in his pocket that morning. He handed it to the woman behind the counter. "Two chocolate bars, please."

"Two chocolate, two dollar," said the woman.

A whole dollar for a candy bar! "I'll take just one," Billy told her.

He stepped out on the porch, wondering where Paul was. Then he saw him some distance away, sitting with his dog on the high bank of the river that served as Kuliknik's highway. Billy walked over and held out his hand for the dog to sniff.

"This is Koolaa. Means 'Poor One.' " Paul gazed proudly at the animal. "He was the runt of his litter, but I knew he would be a good dog."

Billy nodded. Koolaa was a beautiful dog. But they hadn't come to Kuliknik to play with Koolaa. He broke his candy bar in two and gave half of it to Paul. "We won't have much time to look for evidence against Bede Paxton," he said in a low voice. "How do you think we should start?"

"Maybe just walk around town, keep our eyes open," Paul suggested. They walked over to the cabin where the old man was still stirring his kettle of dog food. Paul left Koolaa there. "I'll come back," he whispered to his dog.

They ambled down the street. Paul pointed out a larger building on a rise beyond the scattered houses. "That's the schoolhouse. It used to be the church, too. There's the new church." He pointed to a small, still unpainted, building.

A boy about their age lounged against a woodpile beside one of the houses. "There's my friend Tim. Hey, Tim!" Billy followed Paul toward the boy.

"Hey, Tim. It's me, Paul." The other boy straightened a little, weaving unsteadily. His dark eyes under the unkempt black bangs didn't seem to focus.

"Pa-aul? Washn't las' night a blast, man?"

Billy could see that Tim didn't really know to whom he was talking. The unmistakable smell of booze hung in the air.

Paul whirled away, heading at a near-run toward

125

the schoolhouse. Dropping to the steps, he slammed one fist against his thigh. "Bede Paxton did that. Or somebody like him." Paul's face twisted in anger. "Tim was my friend. He's only fourteen . . . and look at him!"

"But . . . Paxton wouldn't dare smuggle more liquor to Kuliknik after he was busted, would he?"

"I don't know. But I know how we might find out something."

"How?"

"The man who has my dog said Old Josie wanted to see me if I came back to Kuliknik. She has something that belonged to my dad."

"Who's Old Josie? And how could she help us find out about Paxton?"

Paul looked around. No one was in sight, except for Tim, lolling against the woodpile half a block away, but he lowered his voice anyway.

"My dad went to see Old Josie the night he died. She is my grandmother's sister. Everybody likes her. But I think she might be the one who sold Dad whiskey."

"You mean she's the bootlegger?"

"Maybe."

Old Josie called, "Come," in answer to Paul's knock. The cabin seemed dark after the brightness of outdoors. As his eyes adjusted to the dimness, Billy became aware of a bare-board floor. Dozens of faded pictures and knickknacks sat on shelves above a worn sofa. Old Josie herself overflowed the straight chair in

which she sat working at an oilcloth-covered table. Her round face creased with dozens of smile lines at the sight of Paul.

"You come back. City life no good?" With a grunt, she pushed herself to her feet, shoving aside the work she had been doing. Billy saw a strip of leather covered with intricate floral designs made of tiny beads. A flat box divided into compartments held sparkling beads of many colors.

"I make tea. You tell Old Josie about city." The old lady shuffled to the wood-burning stove. She moved a tea kettle toward the front. "Who your red-head friend, Paul?"

"Billy Skarson. I live with his uncle in Fairbanks."

"You see Koolaa?"

"Yes. Joseph told me you have something for me."

"After tea. No hurry."

She put tea bags in three chipped mugs, poured hot water over them, and put soda crackers on a saucer.

Billy tasted the bitter tea. Old Josie chuckled at his expression, and pushed the sugar bowl toward him.

Paul told the old lady about his new home, and school, and about the camp. Billy tried to look around the little house without staring. If Old Josie really was a bootlegger, she didn't have much room to conceal her wares. The entry porch had room only for coats and boots along the sides. Furniture crowded the living area. No room there. A partition hid a small space behind the cookstove. He could see the end of a high, homemade bed, with blankets hanging to the floor. A person *could* store a lot of stuff under there.

"Good tea. Thank you," said Paul.

Old Josie went into her bedroom. She brought back a moosehide carrying bag which she handed to Paul. "This your father's. It was out there," motioning toward the entryway. "Under pile of other things. Found it after you went to Fairbanks."

The boys said good-bye to the old woman. They walked past the store with the bag. Uncle Jess was still talking inside, so they wandered back toward the airstrip. Not far from the metal shed they sat down in the tall grass beneath some willow trees.

"My dad's bag, all right. I remember my mother sewing this." Paul's fingers traced the band of beadwork across the flap. He loosed the strip of rawhide which held it closed. The bag was empty, except for several comic books and a small sack of hard candy. Paul brushed his hand across his eyes. "Presents, for me."

Billy turned so Paul wouldn't see his face. He understood Paul's feelings, but he was disappointed too. Nothing there to help their case against Bede Paxton. He didn't know what he'd expected the bag to hold, certainly not comics.

"Want to read one?" Paul asked.

"Guess so. Nothing else to do right now." Billy leafed through a Superman book. A slip of paper fluttered to the ground. He reached for it; then gasped like he'd been struck in the stomach.

"Paul! Look at this. It's got Paxton's name on it!"

The paper seemed to be a receipt of some kind . . . with the name of a Fairbanks liquor store at the top and Bede Paxton's signature at the bottom. With trembling hands he turned it over. On the back some words were scribbled. He read them out loud.

"I.O.U. $25 to Josie Tom. Signed, James Moses." Under that was a date, the word "Paid," and Josie's signature.

Paul looked closely at the paper. "Old Josie must have used the first piece of paper she picked up for this I.O.U. When Dad paid his bill, she gave it to him."

"Probably. Paul, don't you see? This might be the proof we need that Paxton brought liquor to Kuliknik. How else would Josie have this paper?"

Engrossed in their discovery, the boys didn't notice the small plane approaching the runway until it touched down. Billy started to get up, intending to show their find to Uncle Jess, but something held him back. He crouched in the tall grass. "Let's watch the plane come in."

The plane rolled up to the metal shed. A short, powerfully built man climbed out and began to unload some freight. He swung around to set another box carefully on the ground. For a moment, they saw his swarthy face clearly. "Bede Paxton!" gasped Billy.

Good Riddance to Bede Paxton

Paxton's head jerked toward them. Billy froze. The man's gaze bored into the tall grass where they hid, then slowly moved on across the end of the runway.

They watched the freight agent step out of the metal shed. "Naw, just leave it here," Paxton replied to his offer of help. "I'll get someone to come after it."

"Sure you can manage? I'm going for a cup of coffee then." The agent's dirt bike sputtered toward the village.

Bede Paxton unloaded more boxes. With a last look around, he hiked after the agent.

Billy cautiously raised his head.

"Come on. Let's see what's in the boxes."

"What if someone spots us?"

"They won't. Pretend we're looking for the freight agent."

Paul swung his father's carrying bag over his shoulder. Nonchalantly, the boys sauntered along the runway. They peered into the shed as if looking for someone.

A quick glance toward the village showed no one in sight. Billy ambled toward the plane.

"Quick, Paul, check one of the boxes while I keep watch."

Paul opened his jackknife while pretending to drop his bag. He quickly slit the tape on one box. Lifting a flap, he looked inside.

"Whiskey, all right."

Billy kept his eyes on the village. A woman came out of her house with a broom in hand. Two boys chased each other into the store and out again.

"Let's go." Heart hammering, Billy started toward the houses. Perspiration rolled down his face. Don't panic. Think, he told himself.

Paul spoke. "Better get Officer Jackson."

"Uncle Jess, too. But what about Old Josie?"

"Don't know. She's my relative. But if she sells the liquor for Paxton, she's guilty, too."

Billy nodded. Still, he didn't want to see the old woman in prison.

The two pastors stepped out of the general store just as the boys came up. "Uncle Jess," Billy whispered urgently, "can you get the village safety-patrol officer somewhere where we can talk to him? Bede Paxton's here—with whiskey."

Pastor Black looked hard at the two boys. He gestured with his head in the direction of the schoolhouse. Without a word, he stepped back into the store.

Uncle Jess caught his meaning. "Come on, boys."

The three of them walked casually past the village

132

cabins to the schoolhouse. No one was inside. They sat on the battered desktops to wait.

The Indian officer came in. "You wanted to see me?"

Quickly Jess and the boys explained the smuggling scheme.

"We watched Bede unload his cargo. We checked—he's got whiskey in one box, at least. We heard him say he would get someone to carry it into town."

"Wait here for me." Officer Jackson left to get a search warrant from his office in the cabin that served as the village jail.

"Uncle Jess, what will happen to Old Josie if she really is the bootlegger?"

"I know what will happen," Paul said. "The villagers will make her go somewhere else."

Leave her village? What would happen to the old lady then? Josie was such a grandmotherly sort of person, not Billy's idea of a criminal at all. His excitement at Paxton's soon-to-happen comeuppance tangled with a sick feeling about the nice old woman who would be punished too.

A little boy stuck his head into the schoolhouse. "Pastor Cassidy, come to store."

They all followed the messenger to Officer Jackson.

"Pastor Cassidy, can you go on about your business as if nothing is wrong, but still keep an eye on Josie's place? I need a witness if liquor is delivered to her. Paul and Billy, you come with me. If Paxton sees any of you, he'll take his cargo and get out of here."

At the officer's suggestion, Paul and Billy climbed down the steep river bank, so they were hidden from

133

anyone in the village. They followed the river's edge until they came to the trees between the airstrip and the river. Then they scrambled up the bank and cut through the willows until they could see across the clearing.

From inside the open door of the shed, Officer Jackson signaled them to get down, then ducked back out of sight. Billy and Paul hit the ground together. They'd both seen the dilapidated pickup growling toward the airstrip.

It clattered to a halt between the plane and the shed. From their hiding place, the boys watched Old Josie pull herself from behind the steering wheel. Bede Paxton came round to show her the contents of the top box.

Billy held his breath as Paxton bent to peer at the box Paul had opened, then looked around, puzzled.

Old Josie seemed angry. She folded her arms stubbornly across her ample front.

Paxton turned to face her. "I know you said you didn't want any more. But I've gotta have some cash. The cops have my plane, business is bad . . ."

She shook her head emphatically. Like a locomotive with a full head of steam, she headed for her pickup.

Bede's threatening voice came clearly across the dusty airstrip. "You sell this for me, or I'll turn you in to the town officer. You know what happens to bootleggers. Who'd take you in if you get thrown out of Kuliknik?"

Even from where they crouched in the brush, the boys could see Josie deflate. Glowering, she watched

134

Bede load the boxes into her truck. She snatched the piece of paper Bede handed her to sign.

At that moment, Officer Jackson stepped out of the shed. His voice rang out.

"Bede Paxton, you're under arrest for illegal sale of alcohol in this village."

Paxton lunged toward the officer. The two men went down in a thrashing heap. The boys dashed toward them.

"Josie, go get help!" shouted Paul. The old lady squirmed behind the wheel. The engine ground, turned over. The truck bounced away down the lane.

Paxton was heavier, the more powerful of the two men. He came up on top, pinning one of the Indian's arms with a knee. He struggled to hold the other arm down. Still running, Billy saw a flash of metal as Paxton's free hand yanked a knife from inside his jacket.

Paxton lifted the weapon high. Without stopping to think, Billy leaped toward the upraised arm, putting all his weight into a slashing blow with the side of his own arm. As if in slow motion, he saw the knife arc through the air.

Then he, too, rolled on the ground. He came to his feet and kicked the knife away from the two men. His action gave Officer Jackson the chance he needed. Panting, the officer hoisted the smuggler to his feet by twisting his arm behind his back.

Billy felt a tremendous ache in his own forearm. He heard shouts from the village.

Suddenly, Bede Paxton broke free from the officer's grip. Paul scrambled out of the way as Paxton leaped

for the plane and slammed the door. Billy saw the smuggler's face grow anxious, then angry, as he groped around the cockpit.

Out of the corner of his eye, he caught a sly smile on Paul's face as he passed something to Officer Jackson. Then the freight agent rode up on his dirt bike. Right behind came Old Josie in her pickup, Uncle Jess hanging to the side. Their pilot and a crowd of villagers spilled up the lane from the town.

Officer Jackson brushed the dirt from his clothing and grinned. "You're not going anywhere without this, Paxton." He held up the key Paul had handed him.

Paxton glared down at the people surrounding the plane. He jumped to the ground, shooting a look of pure poison toward the boys.

Jackson pocketed the key. "Thanks, guys. We'll keep this fellow in the village jail until the troopers get here."

"Lock up those boxes until I get back to take care of them, will you?" Officer Jackson asked the agent. "The excitement's over, everybody."

A handcuffed Paxton walked sullenly ahead of the officer to the jail.

Old Josie's wrinkled face sagged like a brown paper bag left out in the rain. "Paul . . . your dad good man. My fault he die. I never mean anyone get hurt."

Paul patted the old woman's arm. "It's Bede Paxton's fault, too. And my dad's. It's over now."

Billy, Paul, and Uncle Jess watched Josie's truck disappear among the cabins of Kuliknik. Dan, the pilot, appeared at their sides just as a cool breeze swept across the airstrip.

137

"Uh, oh. Here comes the weather front the radio warned about. We'd better get out of here." As Dan spoke, a bank of clouds edged across the sun.

Paul looked at the pilot, then toward the village. Billy caught a flash of disappointment in his friend's eyes. Paul hid it quickly, but Uncle Jess had seen, too.

"Something wrong, Paul?" he asked.

"It's okay."

"Come on, out with it."

"Koolaa . . . I didn't say good-bye."

Pilot Dan and the pastor exchanged glances. "I was going to keep this for a surprise, but I'll tell you now, Paul. Dan says that on the first trip out here, when he has extra room, he'll bring Koolaa to Fairbanks. He can stay with my sled dogs. How does that sound?"

Paul couldn't say a word, but his face lit with a twelve-volt grin. He and Billy hopped into the back of the Piper Cherokee. The men took their places in the front.

The little plane taxied to the end of the runway, then accelerated to a take-off past the villagers still standing on the airstrip.

Cloud streamers drifted by the windows. Soon they were climbing between fantastic castles of shining white.

"Tell me, Billy," shouted the pilot over the roar of the motor, "does this kind of excitement happen everywhere you go?"

"I sure hope not. Paxton meant to kill Officer Jackson with that knife." He rubbed the bruise on his forearm.

"Yes, and he could have killed you," put in Uncle

138

Jess. "But Paxton cooked his goose this time. Besides the earlier charges, he's got assault on a peace officer with a deadly weapon, more smuggling charges, and the attempted blackmail of Old Josie. I don't think there's any more to fear from Mr. Bede Paxton, thanks to you boys."

"What will happen to Old Josie?"

"The officer will testify that Paxton threatened her. I hope the villagers will decide she can stay."

Billy sat back, satisfied. He'd helped stop the man responsible for so much unhappiness.

The plane droned on above the sunlit clouds. Both men kept peering out the windows, but no break in the fleecy blanket appeared. After a long time, Dan spoke to Jess. He pointed.

The plane banked sharply. The outside wing tilted up, the inside one down. Instead of straightening, Dan held the turn. Around and down they went in a tight spiral. Billy felt dizzy. His stomach tried to turn inside out. What was wrong?

Then he glimpsed an opening below them like a hole in a doughnut, a patch of green at the bottom. As the plane corkscrewed down through the hole, Billy fought to control his stomach. Just in time, Dan leveled out beneath the clouds. Off to the right, the Tanana River looped across the flats.

Dan turned in his seat. "Better than a carnival ride, wasn't it? Lucky we found that hole. Now you know why fliers take the weather report seriously."

The next few days passed quickly in preparation

139

for the first week of camp. Meanwhile, the judge set a new hearing date for Bede Paxton, one that would allow Billy to testify before his week in Alaska ended.

Camp opened with parents, campers, and little brothers and sisters swarming through the gate. Billy helped to carry sleeping bags and suitcases to the cabins on the hillside. One chubby redhead, lips quivering, stood watching his parents' car bounce away under the "Aurora Borealis Bible Camp" sign. The boy reminded Billy of himself a few years back.

"Hey, would you like to see the boats?"

"I guess so."

He led the child to the dock where Rolf repaired a splintered place on the side of a rowboat. "Rolf's the camp recreation director," Billy told the smaller boy.

The new camper looked interested. "I've never been in a boat," he said. He glanced toward a group of boys near the chapel. "There's my friend Jon," he cried. "I didn't know *he* was coming! See you later." He scurried away.

Rolf chuckled. "Here, I'm finished. Can you give me a hand?"

The two of them wrestled the heavy rowboat over the edge of the dock.

"This is great, man!" Rolf threw his arms wide as if to embrace the lake, the blue sky, the camp buildings on the slope. He held his head high, his shoulders back. His eyes sparkled. He looked nothing like the scroungy, sulking wild man of three short months ago. "Even if the judge lets Paxton go, I'm not scared of him anymore. I realize I've got other choices now." He thrust his hand

140

out to Billy. "Thanks, pal. You and your uncle . . . you're something special!"

Billy felt his face turning red. "I didn't do anything . . ." he started to protest, but just then Corky bounded onto the dock, pursued by two younger campers.

"Whoa!" Rolf grabbed the three. "Rule Number One. No running on the dock."

"Sure, Rolf. Sorry. Hey, Billy, good to have you back." Corky waved cheerfully as he herded the smaller boys back to shore. They dodged around a group of little Indian girls coming down the hill with Susie, their assistant counselor. Two of them, about eight years old, held tightly to her hands as they stopped to look into the chapel. Billy recognized the two little girls he'd seen on the porch of the Kuliknik General Store. Susie flashed him a smile as he and Rolf headed toward the mess hall.

Not only was Rolf different; so was Susie. Billy remembered the unkind remarks she'd made to Paul last spring. Now she was working with Indian children. He squirmed a bit as he remembered his own early dislike of Paul. He'd learned a few things, too.

A couple of days later, an evening breeze ruffled the surface of Half-Moon Lake, blowing away the mosquitoes that usually buzzed around their heads. From a canoe, Billy and Paul watched the midnight sun cast its rosy light over the woods. In camp, the lights-out bell had sounded. Funny, thought Billy. No one could turn the sun out. Not until August would there be any real dark.

141

Tomorrow he and Paul and Rolf and Uncle Jess were to testify at Bede Paxton's hearing. And then he'd have to leave. Horrified, he heard himself sniff. Paul turned to look over his shoulder.

"Must be getting a cold." Billy attempted a grin. "Thanks for showing me how to paddle the canoe, Paul. And for all the other things you've taught me. I'm going to miss you . . . and all the others."

"I learned from you, too," Paul replied seriously. "You and Pastor Jess helped me see I can be somebody. And I saw how you trust God. Now I want to get an education. When I grow up, I want to help my people."

A flash of white swooped over their heads and soared skyward.

"Arctic tern," Paul whispered.

The graceful pointed wings scarcely seemed to beat as the bird described upward loops far above them. A second bird joined the first, soaring high, almost out of sight. The two dots came together, then began a downward spiral, looping, soaring, descending in a breathtaking aerial ballet.

Billy's memory snapped a photograph of white-and-pale gray against the evening blue. Black caps, red bills, long forked tails . . . almost to the water they dived, then lifted clean and flew away to the north.

"They're on their way to the nesting grounds on the North Slope," said Paul.

"Arctic terns . . . aren't they the birds that fly all the way from the Antarctic to the Arctic every year?"

"Yes."

Billy thought about that. Do they really know where they're going when they start that long journey

142

each spring, or do they just follow the program God puts inside them? Paul's decided to help his people. Rolf says he's got choices; he's not afraid anymore. Does God have a plan in mind for me, too?

Billy smiled as the idea grew. Maybe I'm like the terns. Maybe I'll come north again. To Half-Moon Lake. Or wherever God has a job for me to do.